TREASURE HUNTERS

Deep Waters

E. A. House

EPIC Escape

An Imprint of EPIC Press
abdopublishing.com

Deep Waters
Treasure Hunters: Book #4

Written by E. A. House

Copyright © 2018 by Abdo Consulting Group, Inc.

Published by EPIC Press™
PO Box 398166
Minneapolis, MN 55439

Cover design by Laura Mitchell
Images for cover art obtained from iStock and Shutterstock
Edited by Ryan Hume

LIBRARY OF CONGRESS CATALOGING-IN-PUBLICATION DATA
Names: House, E.A., author.
Title: Deep waters/ by E.A. House
Description: Minneapolis, MN : EPIC Press, 2018 | Series: Treasure hunters; #4
Summary: Chris and Carrie have the location of the lost treasure ship *San Telmo*. With
    their friend Professor Griffin and two slightly sketchy grad students, they're off to find it.
    Meanwhile, Maddison's dad has dragged her off to Nebraska, to consult with a retired police
    detective about the disappearance of an old college friend.
Identifiers: LCCN 2017949810 | ISBN 9781680768794 (lib. bdg.)
    | ISBN 9781680768930 (ebook)
Subjects: LCSH: Adventure stories—Fiction. | Code and cipher stories—Fiction.
    | Family secrets—Fiction. | Treasure troves—Fiction | Young adult fiction.
Classification: DDC [FIC]—dc23
LC record available at http://lccn.loc.gov/2017949810

For all my English teachers, who made this happen

Chapter One

"The sky had been calm, but on the night of the twenty-third a wind came in from the east, bringing with it heavy rains and stirring the seas into a mad frenzy," Father Michaels read. He was reading from the parish register itself; the translation he'd written out on a yellow legal pad was lying on Carrie Kingsolver's lap, forgotten. "The will of our Lord, or of some darker being, caused the fleet of Our Majesty the King to be passing by the tip of our island as the worst of the deluge broke, and I witnessed the breaking of seventeen ships upon the unforgiving shores of the nearby islands. Four I saw crumble on the cliffs of

St. Juan. Seven, I saw succumb to the waves in open ocean, five were blown beyond the eyes of this your servant, and one, poor souls, made it nearly to shore before the deluge claimed it on the farthest edge of this island, where the white cliffs look over the waters thick with mussels. The prow of this ship bore an octopus and it was trimmed in red, and I pray that I may offer some relief to the families of the sailors lost to the waves upon her deck."

Father Michaels closed the register, leaving a single strip of acid-free paper in as a bookmark. "It's rough," he said. "It's been a while since I needed to do much Latin translation and there are some variations from the priest's native Spanish that complicated things, but the bit about the octopus is suggestive."

"The prow of the *San Telmo* was decorated by an octopus," Carrie agreed, fiddling with the corner of the translation. Father Michaels was being extraordinarily helpful and the translation he had produced, only a week after being asked, was just about all Carrie could have hoped for, but she still felt exposed and adrift sitting there in the rectory without Chris to ask awkward questions.

Chris had begged off visiting Father Michaels with the excuse that he had a job application he needed to fill out, which was either a blatant lie or a symptom of just how hard Maddison's leaving had hit Chris. Carrie had not had time to decide. He was moping, but that was to be expected. The question was mostly what direction his moping was going to go—would he decide to throw all his energy into the search for the *San Telmo*, or would he decide to try pretending it had never existed in the first place? Although Carrie was usually the only one who ever tried to pretend things never happened. Chris got more and more attached to something the harder you tried to discourage him, and the harder you tried the more *obvious* he made it that he was still on the problem.

"Carrie?" Father Michaels said, and Carrie abruptly realized she'd zoned out. The priest was looking at her with some concern. "Is everything all right?"

"Yes!" Carrie said, and then inwardly winced at

how fake she had sounded. Luckily Father Michaels was kind enough not to press the issue, and instead pushed the register across the coffee table to her.

"Well, as I was saying," he said, deftly removing a cat from the side table and shaking cat hairs off of a map. "That's the only part of the parish register that mentions the wreck. I did skim the rest, but it seems that witnessing the wreck was terrible enough that Father Gonzalez did his best never to mention it again. What *is* interesting is that description of white cliffs and mussels, because . . . "

"Archer's Grove used to have white cliffs somewhere?" Carrie asked. White cliffs put her in mind of Dover Castle and the English Channel, not Florida. But there *were* some endangered mussels that grew almost exclusively on Archer's Grove . . .

"I honestly don't know," Father Michaels said. "But they sound as though they might be a landmark of sorts, so if you were going looking, that would be a good place to start."

"Huh," Carrie said.

"Only about a quarter of the island is the right place for sand marshes," Father Michaels added, spreading out the map, which proved to be a geological map of the island. "It narrows down your search a bit."

"So if there's a point on the island that once had white cliffs and currently has beds of mussels . . . " Carrie said thoughtfully. "You don't happen to know anything about the history of the geography of this island, do you?" she asked.

Father Michaels shook his head. "I'm afraid not," he said. "I studied divinity in school, with a minor in Greek and Latin, so if you wanted to know about the religious history of the island I could help, but not the mineral composition of the island."

Carrie sighed and started gathering up the translation Father Michaels had given her. It looked like she was going to spend the rest of the week in the library. "Anyway, thank you for translating this for us," she started to say—

Her phone buzzed.

"Sorry," Carrie said, and fished it out of her bag.

Ask Fr. Michaels about the dead body, Chris had texted her. Carrie winced and stuffed the phone back into the pocket of her sweatshirt.

"Everything okay?" Father Michaels asked.

"Ah, yeah," Carrie said, trying to hit the N and O keys without looking. "It's just a wrong"—her phone buzzed again. Cringing, Carrie tugged it out of her pocket far enough to see that Chris had responded:

On?

And then, ASK about the dead BODY!!

"Give it a *rest*, Chris," Carrie muttered, and savagely texted back, NO.

"I'm a bit surprised your cousin hasn't called me yet to ask about the dead body in the cistern," Father Michaels said conversationally, and Carrie was so startled she dropped her phone. The priest blinked, then added, "Was that what he was texting you about?"

"You really don't have to tell us," Carrie said. "Chris is a little, um, paranoid right now."

"There actually isn't a lot I can tell you," Father

10

Michaels said. "Despite what always happens in TV crime dramas, DNA testing and fingerprinting take a while with an unidentified corpse, even *if* the faint possibility exists that it might be the body of Cesar Francisco." He crossed his arms thoughtfully. "I did get a call from the local FBI office asking for the names of any pastors here during the fifties and sixties, so I assume they're looking into that angle."

"So they think he was murdered?" Carrie asked.

"Well," Father Michaels said, "and I apologize if this brings up disturbing memories, but when you saw the corpse, do you remember how well preserved it was?"

"It looked fine except for the . . . " Carrie swallowed. "The skull." The skull, in fact, had had a nice, large jagged hole in the back when Carrie had caught a glimpse of the corpse as it was being moved.

"And even in the sixties there wasn't a good way for someone to find their way into that cistern and die accidentally," Father Michaels said. "The problem is that I have no idea *who* owned the skeleton in the cistern." He sighed. "For all we know it could simply be an unfortunate soul who was seeking sanctuary, although—" He stopped himself.

"What?" Carrie asked.

"Oh, it's nothing," Father Michaels said.

"But . . . " Carrie pressed, since in her experience when someone said that it was nothing, they actually meant that it was *something* but they didn't want to bring it up.

"Well . . . I gathered, from the last time I met you, that it's Miss McRae who's an expert on ghosts, but you've probably heard that finding the body and affording the ghost a proper burial is one way to quiet a haunting."

"Yeah?"

"I find it a little worrying that we've had *more* activity in the church since the body was found."

Only a few miles away, a plain black car pulled into

the Archer's Grove police station, and the blond man driving it tucked a slim wallet and a badge that flashed in the sunlight into his suit jacket as he got out of the car. He left a small stack of brown file folders on the passenger seat as he went inside to introduce himself to the chief of police, and if anyone had happened to glance at them they would have been very puzzled by the contents. They were not at all related to the very old disappearance of Cesar Francisco. Instead, the first file held photographs of three high school students and a television star, and the rest were simply full of blank paper.

"Chris," Carrie said while she was halfway through his bedroom window, ignoring the yelp he gave when she started talking, "has it ever occurred to you that asking priests about dead bodies is both a horror-movie-cliché and disturbingly unnecessary?"

"Did he know anything?" Chris asked in response,

and Carrie sat down in her cousin's desk chair with a glare for him.

"No," Carrie said. "The FBI asked him about the pastors of the church in the fifties and sixties—"

"One of them was a radical," Chris offered.

"I don't even want to *know* how you know that," Carrie said. "He suspects the person was murdered, which he *very kindly did not have to tell me but told me anyway*." Carrie paused to poke Chris in the shoulder for emphasis. "He has no more idea than we do who it is. Oh, and . . . the ghostly activity hasn't really died down."

"Huh," Chris said. He ran both hands through his hair, which did nothing to alter his appearance, since he currently looked as though he'd stuck his finger in an electrical socket. "Well, I did the FBI one better," he added, handing Carrie a sheaf of papers. Many of them were missing-persons flyers. "I went through all reported disappearances in the past seventy years."

"And found?" Carrie asked, flipping through the papers. At least Chris had sorted them by decade, although it was unsettling to see how many people had disappeared in the area in the past almost-century.

"Nothing," Chris admitted. "Well, nothing that looked like it had anything to do with the church, or the ship, or—what is it?"

Carrie had paused. There was something about the church . . . and . . . lists? It was hovering just at the edge of her memory—there was something weird about the church and lists of people . . .

"Did something happen in the nineties?" Chris asked, tugging the stack of missing-persons flyers away from Carrie. "Did you see one of these names at the church today?"

"Names . . . " Carrie murmured as the memory formed. "Chris! Did you look at the visitors' log in the church entryway the last time we were there?"

"Yeah," Chris said. "I mean, I didn't read the whole thing but I glanced at it?"

"Did you notice—it goes all the way back to the forties," Carrie said, "but at some point somebody tore out the three pages that would have been the 1990s."

"Yeah, I did," Chris said. "Wait—Carrie, that might mean—"

"I know!" Carrie said. "I looked at it for a really long time when we were hanging out in the entryway waiting for Dr. McRae, but it didn't occur to me to wonder why those pages, and only those pages, were missing!"

Chris put the three missing-persons flyers from the nineties on his bed, lining them up in order of disappearance. There had been an Emily Adderson who had last been seen leaving a local bar on February tenth, a Ryan Moore who had disappeared from his dorm room at Florida State in early October, and a Benjamin Coors—just seven—who had disappeared from his front yard.

"I don't think Benjamin is the right person," Chris said. "He couldn't possibly be the dead body and I don't know why he would be in the visitors' log at a church. But maybe Emily Adderson or Ryan Moore?"

"Yeah," Carrie said. "But how do you find out who signed a visitors' log in a Catholic church over ten years ago when the visitors' log itself has been tampered with?"

Outside in the driveway, a jeep gave a cheerful blat of its horn.

"And do we even want to go down this road?" Carrie added, as Chris looked out the window and then started gathering papers. "I mean, if we want to go with the professor . . . "

Professor Griffin was gratifyingly enthusiastic about the idea of taking Chris and Carrie with him on his next sea voyage. As the only full-time and fully qualified oceanography professor at the local branch of the college, Professor Griffin spent time on the open ocean, in the shallows, in the Everglades, occasionally in tide pools, and generally wherever the current oceanography graduate students needed to be in order to complete their particular concentrated area of study. At the moment he was at loose ends, since there were no pressing end-of-year papers and thus no frantic grad students who needed six more soundings and at least one more night of reading ocean currents, so he had time to be the only bright spot in an otherwise confusing and depressing week.

As a result, he dropped by every day to check on Chris and Carrie and to wear down one or both of their sets of parents until they agreed to the boat trip.

"I've got two grad students who need to do some coastal mapping," Professor Griffin explained the evening after Carrie got the translation from Father Michaels. "Deathly boring, to be honest, but Brad and Harvey are immensely interested in coastal erosion and this is for their thesis. It would get the smaller Kingsolvers out of the house for a few days and give me an excuse to take *Moby* along—and if we do *that,* then this is an educational outreach opportunity for the college and one more reason to convince the board to foot the bill for *Moby's* new propeller."

"Willis, I thought you just replaced the propeller," Chris's mom said carefully.

"Er," Professor Griffin said. "Well, you see, there

was an unfortunate incident involving the propeller and a large, well . . . "

"*Moby* ran into another boat again?"

"Yes," Professor Griffin admitted. "But this time it was a freak ocean current, and not something to do with *Moby's* balance."

"Uh-huh," Carrie's dad said. Actually *nobody* really believed Professor Griffin or was the least bit surprised. The fact that the college had a remote-operated submersible would have been impressive if not for how regularly the submersible malfunctioned in creative ways. There had been many, many comments on the fact that the sub must have been named *Moby* because getting it to work correctly was about as likely as Captain Ahab finding the great white whale. Meanwhile, if Professor Griffin could be said to have any blind spot it was his firm belief that *Moby* was a functional piece of equipment.

"How do I know that terrible submersible isn't going to *eat* my child?" Carrie's mom said.

"Chris and Carrie have been around *Moby* before

and nothing terrible happened," Professor Griffin protested. "And they have done trips before, just nothing quite as long."

The truth everyone was dancing around was that Aunt Elsie had been with them on those trips. Aunt Elsie, despite having once been knocked off a boat by *Moby*, managed to keep the peace between the people who adored the submersible and the people who thought it was a curse on all ships that carried it. Clearly, it was up to Carrie to keep the peace now, especially since Chris was badly shaken by Maddison leaving and firmly in the "*Moby* is an amazing piece of technology" camp to boot.

"If we promise to steer very clear of *Moby* would that help?" Carrie asked.

"Oh sweetheart," her mother sighed.

Carrie kicked Chris under the cover of the coffee table. "If we promise not to fall overboard would it help?" Chris asked, kicking Carrie right back.

Carrie's father sighed. Her aunt and uncle shared

one of their "it comes from both sides of the family; we're doomed" looks.

"Well, I suppose . . . " Chris's mom said.

"If you three are very careful . . . " Carrie's dad added, giving Professor Griffin a significant look. " . . . you can go."

"Thank you!" Carrie said, mentally calculating how much digging she still had to do before she got a narrowed idea of where to look for the ship. "When do we leave?"

That question got passed back and forth for the next hour and a half, because the Professor had two grad students who were perfectly ready to leave that night and Chris's parents had been assuming it would be a weekend thing, and by the time they'd agreed to leave mid-morning the next day it was getting quite late and Chris and Carrie had yet to pack.

Then Professor Griffin pulled them aside on his way out the door.

"I didn't want to say anything in front of your parents," he said quietly, "but I need to ask you—do you happen to know where your friend Maddison and her family are? Besides Montana, I mean?"

"No," Chris said, "why?"

"Look, it's most likely just a mix-up or a misunderstanding," Professor Griffin said. "There was an FBI agent at the archive this morning, asking when Dr. McRae would be back in town."

"I don't know," Carrie said. "You were there when her dad picked Maddison up, you heard the same thing we did."

"That's true, I do remember, I was just wondering if you happened to know more, or if Maddison had called either of you . . . " Professor Griffin said.

Carrie's foot was firmly on Chris's. It would be just like him to admit to the not-quite-SOS Maddison had sent them, and something about the way Professor Griffin was asking made Carrie nervous, although all he did was sigh and readjust his hat before wandering off in the direction of his car.

It was probably nothing. Or it was Carrie's bad habit of getting possessive about secrets. Chris insisted she had a habit of overreacting to people who were just trying to help. Carrie tended to counter this observation with the fact that in her experience, people who suddenly popped up and agreed with your ideas at the very end of a research project were just trying to get a good grade without doing any of the work. Chris tended to do research projects at high speed the day before they were due and so had no idea what Carrie was talking about, and Carrie trusted Professor Griffin to have no hidden agendas, but . . .

The professor had always been as changeable and difficult to pin down as the ocean he loved so much, and Carrie had never been able to really tell what he was thinking at any given moment, but recently he had dialed up that tendency up to—and now past—eleven, and Carrie was starting to worry that *he* was worried and trying to hide it. Something about Dr. McRae alarmed Professor Griffin, although whether it was something about Dr. McRae personally or something about the whole situation and Dr. McRae in general that alarmed him, Carrie didn't know. The professor couldn't think Dr. McRae was dangerous (or up to something suspicious), or he'd have warned Chris and Carrie, and the professor clearly liked Maddison—but then why was he acting even odder and jumpier than normal? And how much trouble was Chris going to cause before they found out?

At least Chris waited until Professor Griffin's tail-lights were fading down the street before pulling a knotted purple hair ribbon out of his pocket. Carrie did not want to add Maddison's cryptic warning to the conversation, especially since she hadn't figured out what Maddison had been trying to tell them yet, and by Chris's expression, he hadn't either.

"I haven't magically come up with a new answer for what she was trying to tell us," Carrie said. "But I still don't think it was her dad she was warning us about."

"I know," Chris said. "I haven't got an answer, either. I just wish she'd *call* me. I have no idea what Maddison is doing."

CHAPTER TWO

MADDISON WAS STARING AT A CHICKEN. IT WAS AN especially unintelligent chicken, and chickens, in Maddison's experience, were generally very dumb. But Nebraska in the middle of the summer, and in the midst of an unexpected wave of cool, rainy weather, was green and humid and boring. Gregory Lyndon owned a small farm in the middle of what he claimed was Newtonville and was more accurately nowhere, and Maddison was suffering from a strange combination of nervousness and boredom. It was made even worse by the fact that her phone got almost no reception in this middle-of-nowhere farm, and she was not at all sure that her messages were getting through to Chris and Carrie. So she was currently staring at one of the dozen brown hens that roamed the Lyndons' front meadow and sat in their flower boxes. Maddison was trying to decide what her next step should be and wondering distantly if the chicken was in the process of laying an egg.

Maddison's father's friendship with Gregory Lyndon was one of the many mysteries that had taken on a slightly sinister edge since Maddison had started asking questions about the *San Telmo*. Kevin McRae and Gregory Lyndon had known each other since before Maddison had been born, and, based on a few comments from her mom, had also known each other since before Maddison's parents had even met. But Gregory Lyndon was twenty-five years older than Maddison's father, and a retired police detective. He was—based on the football team he rooted for—originally from Florida, but living in the same state wasn't enough to explain a friendship that had spanned decades, or why Maddison's father had stayed in touch with Mr. Lyndon even after the retired police detective had moved to Nebraska, which he had done when Maddison was two.

Maddison had a growing suspicion that the answer to the puzzle lay in *where* the two had met, but she still hadn't figured out a good way to ask an old family friend, "Were you the police chief in the college town when my father and this oceanography professor I happen to know had some weird and terrible falling-out that's scarred my dad for life, and by the way, did it have anything to do with a ship called the *San Telmo*?" Especially since her father had been suppressing the story for most of her life. Thus, she was trying and failing to engage a chicken in a staring contest, and wondering what to do next.

There was also that picture she had snapped with her phone of the picture her dad had of Carrie, burning a hole in her pocket. Maddison had taken it at the last minute, when she'd ducked into her father's office back home while he was loading suitcases in the car. Maddison couldn't decide how much of the nerves were really a feeling of guilt. An irrational feeling of guilt, she told herself stubbornly. And maybe just a little anger.

Why did her father have a picture of Carrie, obviously taken unawares and clearly tucked away like a secret? What did he feel he couldn't tell Maddison, even after she had *clearly* been threatened by someone chasing the *San Telmo*'s legendary treasure? And for that matter, what had been the purpose of the file folder marked THC? Maddison had barely looked inside, not wanting to invade her father's privacy, but she had seen what looked like maps sketched on graphing paper, a number of equations, a bunch of random pictures, and several sheets of notes in her father's careful handwriting. Lots of pictures, actually. What possible connection could there be between a bunch of photos of random trees, bushes—if Maddison remembered correctly there had even been a harbor—and Carrie?

"You know, I almost wish he hadn't explained

anything at all," Maddison told the chicken, who clucked.

"Now there's a comment I never thought I'd hear from a McRae."

"Mr. Lyndon!" Maddison said, looking up, startled. Retired police chief Gregory Lyndon was a naturally commanding sight; he was tall, with silvering black hair and an air that seemed to say, "Yes, I am in my mid-sixties, but that doesn't mean I can't still punch someone through a wall."

He had, as a young man, played football in college.

Maddison had known him for years and distinctly remembered the last family Christmas card from the Lyndons, which had prominently featured Mr. Lyndon holding his tiny, pink-blanket-wrapped, first-ever grandchild and looking awed and terrified, and she still had to fight the urge to quail.

"Half the truth can give you a worse understanding of what's going on than an actual lie can," she said instead. "*And* it's easier to kid yourself into thinking you're being fair and honest when you really aren't."

"And that," Mr. Lyndon said, "*is* a McRae thing to say." He picked up the chicken, who seemed resigned to her fate, and extracted a fresh brown egg from amongst the pansies. "You have a nesting box," he told the chicken as he replaced her. She ruffled her feathers in offense and hopped out of the flower box to waddle off in the direction of the garden. "I don't know why you insist on using my flower pots."

"I don't think she's very good at planning," Maddison admitted, as they watched the chicken stalk away in a huff. Mr. Lyndon tossed the egg absently from one hand to another and nodded thoughtfully.

"Want to come help me make a start on lunch?" he asked. Maddison almost bowed out—she was busy thinking—but then it occurred to her that, with her dad in town getting the groceries necessary for feeding extra people and her mom and Mrs. Lyndon halfway across the property at the farm pond fishing, she had a perfect opportunity to ask Mr. Lyndon a lot of questions about her dad while chopping onions.

Starting with "What's going on with my dad?" was

probably a little *too* direct, if the way Mr. Lyndon nicked his thumb and cursed was any indication, but Maddison was *tired* of beating around the bush.

"Many things," Mr. Lyndon said, pressing a paper towel to his thumb. "Including a greater level of paranoia than usual. I *knew* he didn't just offer to do a grocery run to be nice."

"My dad almost didn't graduate from college because of something that happened back then," Maddison said to the onions she was chopping. "I'm beginning to wonder if it involves this local oceanography professor and a lost treasure ship nobody's ever been able to find. He won't tell me what it *was*!"

"Oh boy," Mr. Lyndon told the carrots.

"Which would be fine, except I can't keep avoiding the professor, and it's making everything uncomfortable and awkward," Maddison continued. If Mr. Lyndon was going to carefully dance around telling her anything, he was at least going to know why doing so was a very bad idea. "I think—I think that events might be repeating themselves."

She had cut the second onion in half and diced a good quarter of it before Mr. Lyndon spoke again, and when he did it was quietly and to the carrots he had started carefully cutting into slivers.

"Technically," he said, "it's still a cold case. But either you have excellent instincts or people are talking who shouldn't be, because you happen to be nearly right."

Maddison looked up.

"I have a friend in records who knows my interest in the case," Mr. Lyndon said, "and he called me yesterday to say that the paperwork had been pulled. Something about finding a dead body?"

"Case?" Maddison asked. "What kind of case?"

"At the time, missing persons," Mr. Lyndon said. He put the carrot down and looked at her. "With the understanding that this is not something I should be doing . . . "

"Oh, totally understood," Maddison said, before he could get scared off the topic.

"Before you decide that you aren't going to give up

until you either find the truth or get yourself killed looking for it," Mr. Lyndon continued, "I should tell you that it looks to be turning into a murder investigation."

Maddison gulped. *Murder?*

"In early April of 1997, a twenty-year-old biology major from Florida State named Ryan Moore went missing from his dorm room," Mr. Lyndon told her. "The last person said to have seen him was your father, and the two colleagues of mine who were determined to call the disappearance foul play were also determined to prove that your father did it."

"But he didn't," Maddison said. Hoped, really.

"That was never proved one way or the other," Mr. Lyndon said. "Several of his former friends were firmly convinced that he *was* responsible—a Willis Griffin among them, I assume he's the oceanography professor you mentioned, he was majoring in ocean-ography at the time—but we could never establish a motive or a method or even so much as an eyewitness who saw them together. With no other leads the case fizzled out and went cold." He slid his pile of carrots into a bowl and picked up a bottle of salad dressing. "Until now," he added.

"What are you two up to?" Maddison's father asked as he entered the doorway. Startled, Maddison jumped as her father bustled in the door weighed down with shopping bags and began unloading them.

"Carrot salad," Maddison told him as he stuck a gallon of milk in the fridge, and luckily he took her at her word and didn't ask what else they'd been talking about.

It was, after all, *part* of the truth.

She realized the other part of the puzzle at six-twenty-seven the next morning. Maddison hadn't slept well. The thought of her father accused of murder wasn't comforting, even if Mr. Lyndon didn't seem to think he'd been responsible for anything and the case *had* quietly fizzled out. But that didn't mean it would go away quietly *this* time. You could still be *accused* of a crime a second time if you weren't tried for it the first time. What if her father became a person of interest in the case a second time around?

Well, she'd probably end up in another fight with Chris, which was not something to look forward to.

But what kept Maddison up was not just the idea of her father accused of murder, uncomfortable as that might be. It was the nagging feeling that Mr. Lyndon had worded his explanation very carefully, as though there had been a hint somewhere that he wanted her to pick up on, as though there was something he wanted to tell her that he couldn't, in good conscience, come right out and say to her?

. . . I say . . . I will say . . . I have said—I said, Maddison thought. *Why specifically "said"?*

"The last person *said* to have seen him," she announced, trailing blankets behind her into the kitchen. Unlike everyone else in the house, Mr. Lyndon was an early riser. He was sitting at his kitchen island stirring honey into his tea and he didn't look surprised to see Maddison up. Maddison claimed the chair next to him.

"So who *said* they saw my dad with Ryan Moore before he died?" she asked.

"And that's the interesting part," Mr. Lyndon said, as though Maddison hadn't just restarted an earlier conversation, hours after the fact. "Which everyone, including your father, has so far skipped over completely." He blew on his tea. "After he disappeared, the police interviewed everyone who knew Ryan. On the night Ryan disappeared, your father claimed to have been in his room studying, which was of course—"

"Impossible to verify," Maddison said. Mr. Lyndon nodded.

"Naturally enough, we never verified it. *But,* it seems to have escaped the notice of everyone except perhaps your father that of the three people who told us Ryan Moore and Kevin McRae—well, he was actually Kevin Greenwood at the time, not having met your mother—were out hiking together that night, only one actually saw them together. The other two either remembered Griffin saying he saw them together or were honest enough to admit that they couldn't remember how they knew the two boys were out together."

"So, Professor Griffin was the real source of the worst evidence against my dad?" Maddison asked.

"Mm-hmm." Mr. Lyndon nodded into his mug.

"S-so the person who got my dad in trouble all those years ago, theoretically, is the same person who turned back up in his life just as the *San Telmo* came back into his life," Maddison said slowly. "And somebody died because they got too close to the last-known location of the ship."

"The *San Telmo*?" Mr. Lyndon put his mug down, looking curious. And worried.

"It's . . . this long-lost treasure ship," Maddison said, surprised that Mr. Lyndon didn't already know about it. Hadn't she mentioned it to him already? "Dad's mentioned having friends who were looking for it, and I, er, also have a couple friends who were looking for it, and as soon as they started to, weird things started to happen to everyone around them. Especially—*especially when Professor Griffin was around*," Maddison finished, scrambling to her feet and almost tripping on a tangle of blankets.

"Maddison?" Mr. Lyndon asked.

"Can I borrow your home phone?" Maddison asked, frantic. "I have to at least warn them, if Chris and Carrie are going to be on a boat with Professor Griffin like he offered before we left then they need to know about him being involved in this disappearance—"

Mr. Lyndon had already nodded his permission and Maddison was already dialing Chris's number as fast as she could—she misdialed the number the first time and got a dial tone, and had to pull her own phone out to get the number right—and then it rang and rang and rang until it went to voicemail, and the uneasy feeling she'd woken up with and misdiagnosed as worry over her father got worse and worse. So she didn't hear all of what Mr. Lyndon muttered to himself as he dumped his tea down the drain in an apparent fit of sudden disgust with the universe, so she could have been mistaken.

But Maddison would later have cause to wonder, because she could almost swear that Mr. Lyndon had muttered under his breath, among other things, "Of all the things for the Wyzowski kid to be right about."

In the moment, though, Maddison had bigger things to worry about, mainly that after calling Chris she tried Carrie and got the same lack of response, and she almost didn't need to call Chris's mom's phone and ask as calmly and politely as possible where Chris was. Murphy's Law said that the worst thing that could possibly happen had happened, and Murphy's Law told Maddison she was already too late.

"Oh honey, you just missed Chris and Carrie," Mrs. Kingsolver said. "They're spending a few days with Professor Griffin and his grad students. The signal must not be any good out on the water."

"It just figures," Maddison muttered when she'd hung up.

CHAPTER THREE

THE MORNING OF THE SEVENTH WAS THE FIRST DAY of what was hopefully going to be a simple, two-day expedition "not involving any whales or alligators or waterfalls, in case that was a concern," as Professor Griffin had put it before Chris had managed to stop him from babbling away their best chance of finding the *San Telmo*. It was a Wednesday, and it dawned clear and warm and with a very irritated Carrie.

Carrie was very irritated because Chris had turned up on her doorstep half an hour before she was planning to get up. He had his bags packed, an abundance of excited energy, and two sheets of paper with code phrases on them.

"I'm sorry, what?" Carrie asked, glaring at the offending sheet of paper and wondering why her toes were freezing. She'd been up much later than she had meant to and was already irritated with herself because she wasn't as prepared with the directions to the *San Telmo* as she'd hoped to be. And now Chris wanted her to memorize a whole page of utterly meaningless statements?

"That's the whole point," Chris explained. "I was just thinking—"

"Never good news," Carrie grumbled. Her toes, she had just realized, were freezing because she was standing barefoot on the cold garage floor. Carrie's dad had a bad habit of never remembering to lock the outer door to the garage, so Chris had been leaning against the pile of packing boxes inside the garage when Carrie managed to roll out of bed and open the door. Her parents, when Chris had knocked on the door, had mumbled from underneath their covers and refused to get up. Carrie should have been sleeping with earplugs in so she could ignore annoying cousins until a reasonable hour of the morning, but she hadn't, so here they were.

Plus, Chris was on a roll, and refused to be deterred by little things like sleepy indifference. "I was *thinking*," he continued, "that we need a prearranged way to warn each other without tipping off anyone who might be listening. Something we can work into a regular conversation without it sounding weird or suspicious."

"I lost that monkey you gave me," Carrie read at random. "Excuse me while I go to the restroom briefly . . . I never order roast duck . . . did you walk my pet dog, Billy?" She looked up at him. "Chris, I don't want to imagine a conversation where these phrases would make sense!"

"You have actually said 'Excuse me while I go to the restroom briefly,'" Chris pointed out defensively. But credit where credit was due, he didn't call her a walking dictionary like some people did.

"Yes, and that's the only line that might slip by unnoticed," Carrie allowed, scanning the sheet again. Then she went to hand it back to Chris and discovered that there was a half page on the back. "But then it's also the one you could slip up and say accidentally."

"That's because it's the most important one," Chris admitted, and in a particularly Chris sort of way the logic did make sense. Chris wanted "Excuse me while I go to the restroom briefly" to be code for "Something's wrong, we need to get out of here." Of course that meant that at some point Carrie was going to forget and say the phrase in complete sincerity and make Chris panic, and Carrie told him as much.

"I just want us to be able to communicate warnings clearly," Chris said. And he was sincere, and worried, and the idea for code phrases had come to him at nine o'clock the night before and then he had been up half the night putting them together, which meant that he was worried and trying to fix things in the only way he knew how.

"Still worried about what Maddison was trying to warn us about with CQD?" Carrie asked.

"I still can't even get through to her," Chris admitted, and he looked so genuinely worried about Maddison that Carrie sighed and snatched the sheet away when Chris went to take it back.

"No, leave it with me, I'll try to start memorizing it," she said, and Chris lit up like the outside sky hadn't yet. "I'll *try*," Carrie emphasized. "But no panicking if I accidentally warn you of incoming cyclones the next time I try to order an ice-cream cone."

"I don't even have a code word for cyclones!"

✗ ✗ ✗

Professor Griffin's boat—or, as he kept reminding them, his *research vessel*—was named *The Vanishing Triangle*. The reasoning behind the name was Professor Griffin's, and unfathomable, although Chris had occasionally wondered if the professor was trying to make a sideways reference to the Bermuda

Triangle. Carrie kept stopping him before he could actually ask, though.

"It's, I don't know, rude," she told Chris for about the fifth time as they wandered down the harbor, looking for the professor or an unusual amount of startled yelling that might indicate he was trying to load *Moby* onto the *Triangle*.

"How is *mentioning* the Bermuda Triangle rude?" Chris asked. He was curious; he and Carrie had this argument about the possible connection between *The Vanishing Triangle* and the Bermuda Triangle every time they went near the ship. Carrie always told him to stop looking for mystical triangles where there weren't any, but today's objection was a new one.

"You never hear of people ending up in the Bermuda Triangle and having a perfectly uneventful trip," Carrie explained irritably, tugging at her rain jacket. "It's always, 'First the compass failed, and then the fog got so thick we couldn't see, and then something tried to eat the boat.' I don't think it's nice to imply that you can't think of a person's boat without thinking of a place ships go and never come back."

"But we aren't even going *into* the Bermuda Triangle!" Chris protested. True, the Bermuda Triangle was said to exist more-or-less in the area roughly between the tip of Florida, Puerto Rico, and Bermuda, but Professor Griffin's two grad students were studying coastal erosion and Chris and Carrie were looking for the *San Telmo*. There wasn't any coast to study in the Bermuda Triangle. And Carrie was almost sure the *San Telmo* had sunk very near the shore of the island, so their boat was never going to drift into the Bermuda Triangle unless they got very lost.

"Sure, we aren't going into the Bermuda Triangle," Carrie said grimly, coming to a halt in front of *The Vanishing Triangle*. The *Triangle* only had her name on the prow in small lettering and the ship looked aggressively normal, but the action surrounding it was a dead giveaway. A minivan with the college logo on one door was backed up almost far enough to fall off the dock and into the water, *Moby* was hanging suspended from a complicated tangle of cables and pulleys halfway between it and the boat, and Professor Griffin was flitting around and between the two like a little bird on a sandbar. "We might not even need the Bermuda Triangle to make this weird," Carrie finished, just as Professor Griffin looked up and noticed them and waved frantically at . . . *Moby*. The odd little submersible was tilting alarmingly to the left and beginning to spin slightly. *Moby* was a cheerful plastic-and-metal, robot-like unmanned submersible about the size of a milk crate (although much heavier and more unwieldy), with one eye (actually a camera), two LED "headlights," and a claw-arm that was supposed to collect samples from the sea floor but tended instead to get caught in seaweed. Or snagged on one of the cables lowering *Moby* to the deck, as it was now.

"The crane broke again," a voice said from inside the minivan, and Chris and Carrie hurried over and out of the way of the falling submersible to find the professor's TA, Abigail Chang, in the driver's seat, one earbud in and her phone in her lap. She'd been dealing with the professor and with *Moby* for almost three years now and as such was completely unbothered by Professor Griffin and the submersible's regular brushes with disaster.

"And so then he asked the first-year engineering students to 'rig something up for him' last night," Abigail continued. "I'm waiting over here because I do *not* want to lose an eye right in the middle of writing a thirty-page paper on ocean currents."

The crane substitute did look like it was going to pull itself apart if someone snapped the wrong cable.

Moby landed safely and more or less gently on the deck of the *Triangle*, the tangle of cables bouncing free and whipping back and forth wildly. One of the students helping Professor Griffin almost fell into the water. Abigail took the earbud out of her ear and buckled her seatbelt.

"Oh, I'm not coming with you," she explained when Chris gave her a puzzled look. "Too many papers, and I have all my data for wind currents already. I'm just here to help Professor Griffin load *Moby* and then take that . . . thing . . . back to the engineering department when it's done."

"But then who's going on the trip?" Chris asked. Abigail was widely considered to be the reason Professor Griffin and *Moby* hadn't fallen overboard and been lost at sea forever, and Chris had assumed she'd be coming. She liked the sea almost as much as the professor did. And there was the little matter of how Chris knew his parents had caved on the idea of Chris and Carrie being out for a few days with the professor *because* they had assumed Abigail would also be there.

"Who's going on the trip?" Abigail repeated. "Well, you two, Professor Griffin, *Moby* if he doesn't fall over the side, and Brad and Harvey. I don't know the two guys," she explained. "Apparently they're on loan from another college because they needed to do underwater coastal mapping and one of their professors knows Professor Griffin."

"Huh," Chris said. Carrie looked faintly suspicious. Of what, exactly, Chris couldn't say, and then Professor Griffin hurried over to introduce Brad and Harvey as they all struggled to stuff a massive and now hopelessly tangled mess of wires into the back of the van, and by the time they were done and Abigail had left it was half an hour past the point they'd intended to be off and even Carrie was too busy to be suspicious.

The plan—as explained by Professor Griffin while strapping *Moby* securely to the deck in an out-of-the-way corner of the boat—was to circle the island, hugging the coast, and take samples of the water and pictures of the shoreline at regular intervals. Professor Griffin intended to deploy *Moby* at about the halfway point, so Brad and Harvey could take samples of the sediment settling in the waters off the relatively undeveloped half of Archer's Grove.

"So, we'll take the populated side of the island first," the professor had explained, "and then work our way around the state parks side, then back to where we started."

Thanks to its state and national parks Archer's Grove actually had a relatively unspoiled natural side, and it was this natural side that might be hiding the *San Telmo*. The ship had gone down, according to the seventeenth-century missionary priest, within visual range of the old mission church, somewhere under white cliffs and by a mussel bed. Archer's Grove had a few beds of mussels even in modern times. They were protected areas because of the endangered mussels that lived there, and they had been much more widespread before development and a governor who hated mussels had ruined a great many of them. The mussel beds that could have been seen from the mission church, Carrie had discovered, lay near the arrowpoint-shaped tip of the island, amongst its largest state forest.

"But not the cliffs?" Chris asked Carrie in a furious

whisper that afternoon. "You don't know where the cliffs are?" They had finished a late lunch in defiance of a flock of seagulls, and now the professor was supposed to be making sure they didn't hit anything. Harvey and Brad were out on the sliver of exposed deck taking a series of pictures, and Chris had been deathly bored, until he poked his head into the room he and Carrie were sharing and found her frantically poring over books.

"What?" Carrie said. "I'm working on it! I'll get there! It would've been worse to give up the opportunity that the professor dumped in our laps. I'll figure it out!"

Chris was still floored by the idea that *Carrie* had managed to be caught flat-footed and less prepared than she could be. Carrie was the person who did her homework *ahead* of the teacher assigning it. She had once done an entire book report before their second-grade teacher had handed out the book, and she had once broken out in hives at the sight of an overdue assignment. A spelling worksheet from second grade had blown off her front porch and disappeared, and although Carrie had been given a replacement and turned the assignment in on time, she had found the original paper growing mold and mildew in the corner of the garden shed five months later and broken out in hives. Carrie swore up and down that the hives had been from the mold and mildew in the shed, but that didn't make nearly as good a story and so no one believed her. If Carrie wasn't prepared with any kind of research, the world was about to end. Chris said as much, which was a terrible mistake.

"I had to order the book from a library in Wisconsin!" Carrie snapped, throwing the book in question at Chris, "and I don't see *you* helping, Mister Mopey!" There were two different pencils stuck in her messy bun and she had a sticky note clinging to her sleeve. Slow-kindled rage burned in her eyes. It occurred to Chris that he had kind of left Carrie hanging ever since Maddison had left, and that she'd been researching a dozen different subjects to get the location of the *San Telmo* as close as possible, and he resolved to be as contrite as possible. This must have been obvious because Carrie relented. "It only got in yesterday and I haven't had time to go over all the maps," she explained much more quietly, and yanked a book out of her pile and waved it at Chris, who grabbed it and opened the page with the most sticky notes.

"'The mussel beds where *Mytilus Arquitenens* congregate are located at the southern end of the island, where the ocean currents permit a high concentration of salinity and the grasses are seldom disturbed,'" he read.

"I wanted you to look at the pictures," Carrie sighed.

"Oh," Chris said, and then, "*Oh!*" Mussel beds were not just a good place to find endangered mussels, they were supposedly where the *San Telmo* had sunk, and Carrie's copy of *Endangered Floridian Mollusks* had a map that showed the current and past extent of the mussel beds. In full color.

"If I can compare where the beds of mussels were

with where there were supposed to be white limestone cliffs," Carrie said, "and then compare *that* with what you could see from the old Spanish mission church, I ought to be able to tell you where the *San Telmo* went down. I just haven't had a lot of luck finding any maps that show the white cliffs, although three of the books that mentioned them said they were unusual."

"But that's good, because it means finding the cliffs should help narrow everything down," Chris pointed out. He shifted a stack of graphing paper and maps off the bunk that was supposed to be his, and sat down.

"Unless I don't have the books I need to find the cliffs," Carrie groaned. "I couldn't pack everything." Chris raised his eyebrows, because Carrie had probably weighed the boat down with her books more than the professor had with *Moby*, and he was seriously wondering if Carrie had thought to pack a change of clothing and a toothbrush along with the ten books and an uncounted number of maps.

"I couldn't pack everything *that I wanted to*,"

Carrie clarified, tossing to Chris a map on which she had picked out the marshes and the old mission church, along with a circumference of what a reasonable human being could have seen from the mission church. "And I *did* remember my toothbrush, thank you very much. And even my phone, although I'm not getting a signal, so if I do need a book I don't have, I don't know how I'm going to call home and get Dad to read a few pages for me."

Chris had been wondering whom Carrie had found to calculate how far Father Gonzalez could have seen from the mission church on a stormy night and why he didn't know that person, but he jumped and fished his own phone out of his pocket when she mentioned the phone. No service.

"We still have a radio," he said, trying to ignore the small spike of unease. It was the simplest thing in the world to lose phone reception when you were on the ocean—despite what Carrie thought of the Bermuda Triangle, weird things did happen when you were surrounded by a vast blue mystery—and yet it seemed almost too inconvenient. A shipboard radio was all well and good, but no phones meant no contact with the outside world, and no contact with the outside world meant no warnings in or out, if you thought there was a need for warnings. Chris squashed a little trickle of unease with considerable difficulty. They would only be away for two days, and it wasn't as though Maddison had been trying to call him all morning.

Chapter Four

MADDISON ONLY GAVE UP AFTER SPENDING HER whole morning trying to call Chris and getting nowhere. She'd also gotten nothing but sympathetic looks from her parents and even Mr. and Mrs. Lyndon. It was the sympathetic looks that were freaking her out, far more than the lack of contact from Chris or even the cold, hard truth that her father had once been a suspect in a murder investigation. It was impossibly hard to convince yourself that you were overreacting when all the adults in your life were acting like you had a right to be upset.

And it was a missing person case, Maddison told herself fiercely. *Not murder. At least not then.*

After all, there were perfectly good explanations for why the phone was going directly to voicemail, starting with "He dropped it in the water" and going on from there. There didn't have to be anything suspicious going on. There *shouldn't* be anything suspicious going on, and Maddison *shouldn't* be afraid that a respected college professor was going to turn out to have pushed two of her friends over the side of the boat.

Maybe if she called one of their home phones again?

"Maddison, try a different tactic," her mother finally said, interrupting her in the middle of dialing Carrie's parents' number for the sixth time. "You aren't going to get through that way."

"Or get some rest," her father added. "You were up very early this morning."

"Okay!" Maddison said—yelled, really—and took herself back to the bedroom she was staying in, because if nothing else, her mom was right and she could probably stand to get dressed before noon. There were a number of significant looks exchanged as she left, but Maddison was feeling irritable and miserable and out of sorts so she didn't really register them.

It was shaping up to be a pretty day, the gray rain giving way to a clear blue sky with nice puffy clouds and no heat haze, and the Lyndons had given her the prettiest room in the house. It was the topmost room in the house, aside from the attic, and had a white and lavender color scheme, and could be called charming with absolute sincerity. Maddison didn't have time for the white lacey curtains, or the pretty dried flowers on the bedside table, and she went directly to her bed, replaced the covers she'd been carrying around all morning, threw two cross-stitched pillows across the room, and pulled up the pictures on her phone.

Then Maddison felt horribly guilty so she got up and retrieved the cross-stitched pillows and *then* sat back down. The picture of Carrie, taken from a picture in her father's study, gazed up at her, even though the Carrie in the picture was looking away from the camera with her face half hidden in a halo of escaping red hair. Glaring at the picture was a nice substitute for glaring at her dad. Maddison was sure that he had nothing do with the disappearance of some kid he'd gone to school with. She was *absolutely* sure that he hadn't murdered anybody. She knew—she'd known her whole life long—that he always had her best interests at heart.

Didn't she?

The truth was, Maddison wasn't sure. Not of the big things—Maddison forced herself to think it through rationally and she could admit that she didn't believe her father was capable of any kind of murder. He'd gone to much too great a length to keep Maddison and her two friends safe, and not once since this mess had started had he demonstrated any fear for himself. At least, not the kind that might drive him to lash out at another person to protect himself. It had always been fear of something happening to

Maddison that had driven him, and driven him to some really odd actions.

So what, then, was so upsetting about the picture, and by extension, why was she so mad at her dad again? *It's logically upsetting,* Maddison reminded herself. But she had the strange creeping feeling that something wasn't quite right about the picture itself, as though there was something subtly off about Carrie. *Why am I really upset?*

Well, it was an invasion of privacy. Carrie's privacy first of all, because to photograph her unawares was invasive and creepy, especially if you happened to be someone else's dad. And then Maddison's privacy had been invaded, too, since her dad was following her friends around without giving Maddison any say in the matter and the very following-around suggested he didn't trust Maddison to make good decisions.

"I mean, really, what's scary enough about Carrie that he can't just ask me?" Maddison said out loud to herself. "She's a teenage girl, she's not the Spanish Inquisition or a demon clown, there's no need to stalk her like she's going to catch you following her and eat you—oh."

Maybe there wasn't something scary about Carrie, but there was something scaring her dad. He was scared. Her dad was scared, and acting oddly because of it. Overreacting to everything because of it. What, after all, was him dragging them all the way from Florida to Nebraska but him running away and taking the family along with him?

And suddenly, all of Maddison's pent-up frustration over her father's dancing around his past sparked up into a flaming rage. Something terrible had happened to him when he was only barely older than Maddison was now. Okay, she *got* that. But refusing to even mention what had happened when people were *dying* because of it? And trying to keep Maddison safely out of it by keeping her in the dark, far past the point where it got ridiculous? And leaving Chris and Carrie alone, not knowing any of the suspicions Maddison's dad had about Professor Griffin, just so that he could get Maddison away from the guy? Really a bad idea. There was scared, and then there was running away, and seriously, if he thought the situation was so bad it needed to be fled from, why hadn't he told Maddison how bad it actually was?

Maddison got to her feet, threw her phone at the pillow with unnecessary force so that it bounced, and stomped across the room to her open suitcase. If she was going to fight the urge to strangle people she might as well put it to good use and abuse her wardrobe. T-shirts could be thrown with more force than phones or random china cats on the mantelpiece, and they could also be thrown without particular guilt at fathers who dared to knock on Maddison's door when she was simmering with anger.

"Go *away*," Maddison snarled. One of her flip-flops bounced off her dad's chest and fell over the stair railing. Maddison spared one second to admire her aim, and one to feel horrified that she'd thrown a shoe at her own dad, but honestly, right now? Right now he deserved it. "Unless you want to be honest," she added for good measure, "for once in your life, stay *out*!"

Then she flipped her whole suitcase over and threw herself on the bed, fighting the urge to cry, and losing.

Back in Archer's Grove, another plain, black car pulled into the parking lot of the Archer's Grove police station. The two people who got out looked tired and harassed, probably because their flight had been delayed and the DNA results they needed weren't in yet.

"I hate old murder cases," the woman said to the man as she swung her jacket over her shoulders. There was a gun in the holster at her hip.

"I've only got a few minutes," Father Michaels said with the greatest politeness and a certain amount of suspiciousness when the FBI turned up on his door-step, "I'm in the middle of writing my sermon, and I have Mass at four thirty. And if you want to know about the priest here in the fifties I would really recommend getting in touch with my predecessor," he added, which was when the suspicion turned into a certainty, because the blocky young man in a black suit who had waved a badge under Father Michael's nose much too fast for him to actually read it looked confused, and then uncomfortable.

Father Michaels had been the priest at Saint Erasmus for six years, and he'd been chasing away thrill-seekers for every one of those years. He knew his local history, and the top ten most likely identities of the ghost in his cistern, and he knew the life and times of the Cuban revolutionary rumored to have made it to Archer's Grove, bleeding and pursued, before dying and passing into legend. If the body of Cesar Francisco really had been found in the cistern of Saint Erasmus, then the government agency knocking on his door ought to be the CIA.

The FBI suggested that it was murder, or possibly a crime that had crossed state lines, or just that the local police department had decided there was something wrong with the crime scene. Or, as Father Michaels suspected, the FBI wasn't involved in the case at all, and this was a ham-fisted attempt to pump him for information.

"Well then," Father Michaels said kindly to the man on his doorstep, "what kind of questions do you have for me?"

He wasn't very reassured. Agent Simmons was very sorry, but he needed to ask if anyone had borrowed the old church records recently. Asking what kind of old church records—Father Michaels was holding a distant hope that this was a creative way of verifying who'd been in the church basement in the sixties—had resulted in a lot of awkward mumbling, until finally Agent Simmons had resorted to pulling a notebook out of his pocket in order to get the title right and clarify that he'd meant to ask if anyone had come in and asked about the parish registers recently, and if so, could Father Michaels please describe them?

"Is it a matter of life or death?" Father Michaels asked.

"Yes," Agent Simmons said earnestly. Father Michaels didn't believe him for a minute, but as it was the FBI . . .

"I'll need contact information," Father Michaels said. "And I should probably have your badge number as well—I'm happy to cooperate, but if the situation's been misrepresented to me, we're both committing a mortal sin—" *That* got the agent's attention, and he did hand over his badge, so Father Michaels could take down his name and badge number. "I'm afraid I can't tell you all that much," he said to Agent Simmons. "I've had four or five people ask to see the parish register, mostly college-age students. And we don't keep track of that sort of thing unless they want to take a piece of church record out of the rectory. I think most people sign the guest registry, so if you want to look there you're welcome to it."

He showed the agent where the guest registry was, allowed him to take pictures of it, and agreed to call the man if he remembered anything, and then presided over his four-thirty Mass, thinking about his encounter with the agent all the while.

Then Father Michaels tracked down the phone number for the closest FBI field office, locked his door, let the cat in when the cat tried to claw through the door because he'd been sleeping under the statue of Saint Frances in the church, and prepared to spend a fair bit of time explaining himself. It was probably just a misunderstanding, but Father Michaels hadn't forgotten the extremely strange conversation with the new local archivist about who else had asked to see the parish register. The man had seemed to think that his daughter would be in danger from anyone who came around asking about Father Gonzalez and the wreck of the *San Telmo,* and Father Michaels had to agree that the current circumstances were unsettling. He wasn't suspicious by nature, but reportedly haunted churches attracted the odd and alarming and it was usually better to be safe than sorry.

When his call went through, Father Michaels asked the cheerful-voiced switchboard operator if she could please check if someone with this specific badge number was supposed to be going door-to-door asking questions in Archer's Grove.

"Certainly!" the operator said. "Let me see what I can do. Please understand that I may not be able to confirm or deny the actions of our agents if the investigation is ongoing—hmm."

Long experience in dealing with people who didn't want to tell him things, like why the Easter decorating committee was on strike, told Father Michaels he'd be best served by staying silent.

"Just a minute," the switchboard operator said. "Would you please hold while I transfer you?"

He was on hold for a surprisingly short amount of time before someone with a voice perfect for yelling over a megaphone picked up the line.

"My apologies for the wait, Father," she said. "You

are correct, that badge number is faker than my left eye. Would you be able to describe this person?"

✗ ✗ ✗

Bethy Bradlaw was, by temperament, more easily alarmed than Father Michaels. She was also under more stress than the priest, who was not trying to corral a film crew at a harbor while Robin Redd gave in to a childhood fascination with manatees and bounced around like he'd had too much sugar. And she hadn't been forewarned about suspicious people looking for clues to the *San Telmo*. So it took her much longer to realize that the FBI agent who tracked her down at the harbor and approached her in the middle of hammering out last-minute script changes wasn't quite legit.

Of course, another reason Bethy took longer to get suspicious was because Bethy had her own reason to fear law enforcement turning up at her door and asking questions about the week the *Treasure Hunter* crew had just spent in the Pine Lick State Park. Her brother had made a frightening attempt to sabotage his own television show and had nearly shot someone only a few days earlier, and Bethy had been half expecting a police officer at her door ever since. The FBI was worse, but Bethy wasn't exactly surprised, and she spent about half an hour trying to run the guy off without obviously running him off or tipping him off to her brother's whereabouts. Or shoving him off the dock before he could ask any awkward questions about her brother's brief attempt to commit murder.

It was, in fact, only when he proved much more interested in the people her brother had tried to kill than in her brother that Bethy began to wonder where the interview was actually going.

"Look," the federal agent said, pulling a manila envelope out of his briefcase and laying three misshapen pictures on Bethy's rickety card table. It wobbled alarmingly at the addition of new weight, but Bethy had set it up in a tiny puddle of shade so she could guard the boat and, incidentally, get cornered by FBI agents. She was starting to regret sending the rest of the crew to pick up last-minute snacks and essentials. It wasn't as if anyone was actually going to steal the boat. They were renting it for manatee filming and had gotten what they paid for, which was to say, floating death. The boat was listing sideways and was probably going to exceed its weight limit if Robin brought his beloved fiberglass manatee sculpture along, or Bethy relocated to the deck to get away from Agent Simmons.

"Ma'am," Agent Simmons said, dragging Bethy's attention back to the present, "I'm not interested in what your brother did or didn't do on the night of the seventeenth, I'm just interested in whether or not you saw these kids in the woods that day."

"Well, I may have," Bethy said, finally looking at the pictures. The pictures of Chris and Carrie Kingsolver were matching school portraits. The picture of Maddison McRae had been carefully trimmed, but it looked suspiciously like it had been printed off a school website. There was a basketball court in the background and a random extra arm in the picture. It was also an older picture than the others. If all the kids' parents had contributed these photos, Bethy would eat Robin's ridiculous hat.

"It is absolutely essential that we identify their movements over the past three weeks," Agent Simmons said earnestly, with a hint of a dark undertone. "Otherwise we might have to start looking more closely at those who may have seen them. Dragging other incidents into the light."

"I see," said Bethy, who had spent years dealing with bad, stuck-up, just plain overdramatic actors and had never seen a more pathetically heavy-handed threat in all her life. Or a worse portrayal of a federal agent—Bethy had been an extra in an episode of *Bureau,* and she had done a better job herself. She was increasingly less interested in cooperating. "Well, I'll have to go back and go through the release forms from when we were shooting," she said, because she did. "And then I'll need you or somebody from your office to fill out a release form, and there will have to be a signed agreement on what information can be released and what can be withheld or the insurance company will drop us."

"You can't just tell me what I need to know today, and I'll send someone to deal with the paperwork later?" Simmons asked. He was looking at the massive stack of forms Bethy was pulling out of numerous folders with a horrified expression, which Bethy had expected. Massive stacks of paperwork were how Bethy repelled people she couldn't throw out when they were refusing to go away.

"Sorry," Bethy said. "If I tell you anything, then the form has to be signed by you."

That actually alarmed the agent, who suddenly found an excuse to leave without giving Bethy a card in case she needed to contact him. Even more suspicious. She was stuffing paperwork back into folders when Robin Redd turned up, thankfully minus Bill the Fiberglass Manatee, but lugging—*oh horrors*.

"Why do you have a giant *inflatable* manatee?" Bethy asked. "And why is it *purple*?"

"Who was the blond guy?" Redd asked her instead of answering.

"Oh," Bethy sighed, wondering if she could get the folding table to collapse like it was supposed to or if she was going to have to wrestle it back into her car half-erect. "Some wannabe FBI agent who was asking me *highly suspicious* questions about those kids we met on the Annie Six-Fingers shoot."

There was a splash, and the giant inflatable manatee was suddenly bobbing in the water. Redd looked almost more alarmed than the FBI agent had. He'd made a startled movement and apparently the purple inflatable manatee was slippery. "Did he ask you about the *San Telmo*?" Redd asked.

"No—well, he asked if the kids had said the name," Bethy said. "Why, what does this have to do with a seventeenth-century sunken treasure ship— what are you *doing* in my folders?"

"They did leave contact numbers on those release forms you were waving around, right?" Redd asked, shaking out her file of catering contracts. Bethy watched him in alarm. *My poor, poor filing system*, she thought.

"Should I be more worried than I already am?" she asked finally, when Redd had finally found the correct forms and was searching his safari vest for his cell phone. "Or do you have a rational reason for throwing your inflatable manatee in the drink and frantically calling three kids we don't know very well?"

✕ ✕ ✕

Park ranger Helen Kinney was in the middle of coordinating search-and-rescue training in the sandbars, had three reports of marijuana being grown mere meters off a hiking trail to deal with, and needed to check on some potential vandalism to the giant rock that looked exactly like a hand. She looked up from her computer and made grabbing motions at Agent Simmons until he handed over his badge, and then she took one look and threw him out of her office because, she said, "If you want to waste my time pretending to be a federal agent, do it when Old Stoney the rock isn't in danger of being picketed by the committee against public indecency and we haven't lost a search-and-rescue team."

Then she stared for a whole fifty seconds at the door he had flown out of like a man possessed before she sighed and picked up her phone.

"Kevin!" she said when someone picked up. "Glad I caught you—what on earth are you doing in Nebraska? Uh-huh. I don't believe you at all, you know. Anyway, there was a fake federal agent in here asking about illegal hiking . . . "

✕ ✕ ✕

"Let me see your badges?" Father Michaels asked, for the second time in a day and a half. The two people on his stoop, both wearing sensible suits and even more sensible shoes, looked at one another and produced FBI badges that were a little less "second-hand-cobbled-together-thrift-store" in appearance. Father Michaels sighed.

"Okay," he said, holding the door open. "*Please* tell me you aren't here to ask me a lot of strange questions about the church being haunted and who might have looked at the parish registers in the past six years."

The dark-haired woman blinked. Her partner, who had a worryingly orange tie and flyaway blond hair and was clearly newer to this, said, "Wait, what?"

"The conspiracy theories," Father Michaels said. "I was warned about them when I first came to this parish, but to be fair, nobody expects to spend an entire month answering questions about past parish priests who may have buried treasure somewhere in the rectory. I have a sermon to write!"

"We're actually here about the person passing himself off as an agent," the woman said, "and about the body found in the church cistern last week. You said there's an increased interest in buried treasure tied to this parish?"

She did not look as though she was taking this

news lightly. Although it had to be admitted that she didn't look like she took anything lightly: her suit was crisp, her hair was in a severe French braid, and her left eye wasn't quite focused on Father Michaels because it was actually glass. And she didn't look like the type of person to have lost that eye in a simple accident.

"Yes," Father Michaels said. "Supposedly parts of the parish register kept by Father Gonzalez detail where the *San Telmo* went down, and since his mission church became this parish, people come in asking questions about him all the time. It's flared up again recently—I think there must have been a television program about the ship."

"Drat," the woman said under her breath, scribbling something in her notebook. "I was hoping the two cases weren't related."

CHAPTER FIVE

THE PROBLEM WITH SPENDING ANY AMOUNT OF time on a boat, Chris reflected, was that it eventually got so *boring*. You could lean on the deck railing staring at an endless blue horizon for only so long before you got sick of it, and switching to the other side and a view of the coastline chugging past only worked once. Then that got boring and you were stuck, with nothing to do but *not touch* the delicate scientific equipment because the only people allowed to accidentally break pieces off were the professor's grad students, and try to avoid driving your cousin crazy.

Carrie had thrown him out of their shared cabin and barricaded the door when Chris asked her for the fourth time why she thought Maddison wasn't calling him back.

"Either distract yourself or swim home and hitch-hike to Nebraska," she had ordered him irritably through the thin wood, "but leave me alone to finish this!"

"Jeez," Chris had replied, and gone off to stare at the horizon for a while. He'd remembered to pack and take seasickness medication this time, but he still felt a little spacy, and the strange, oppressive tension hanging over the boat wasn't helping matters. Carrie was irritable, Chris was worried about Maddison, the two grad students were unknown factors, and even Professor Griffin was a little nuttier than usual.

"Such a lovely, cruel mistress!" he had announced unexpectedly in the middle of Chris's sea gazing, wandering over to lean lazily on the railing. If the professor was going to keep doing things like this, they were massively lucky the ship had an autopilot and both grad students could steer. Chris and Carrie had enough accumulated experience with boats that they could probably get everyone back to some part of Florida in an emergency and not accidentally end up in Spain, but neither had what you might call practical experience.

"The sea, I mean," Professor Griffin continued, and Chris let him go on, even though the sea had never called to him the same way it did to the professor. It was true that he liked it, that Carrie had pestered a healthy fear of it into him, and that occasionally it made him horribly nauseous, but there wasn't any mystery in the sea on its own. Chris reserved that for the things *in* the sea. Apparently Professor Griffin didn't. "So wide, so poetic," the man went on, spreading his arms out wide. If he tried to reenact the most famous scene from the movie *Titanic* Chris might have to go back to bothering Carrie. "So indifferent to the things we do . . . oh yes," Professor Griffin said when Chris looked up at him. "That's always fascinated me. Do you know the definition of the word *amoral*?"

"Wrong?" Chris asked, caught off guard by what felt like a sudden change of subject.

"Ah, a common mistake. No, that would be immoral. Amoral, with an A—that means something different, something, hmm, deeper. Like the ocean!"

"Okay . . . " The professor was getting philosophical again. This was why Chris tried to bring other people with him when he got stuck with the guy in isolated quarters, especially on the water. The ocean made Professor Griffin massively philosophical, and when he got massively philosophical, Professor Griffin got confusing. Chris gave him a worried, sideways glance.

"Sorry, I was getting carried away," the professor said, taking his captain's hat off to gesture with it and then deciding instead to lean against the railing for a bit. "Amoral means not caring about the right or wrong of a thing, transcending the black and white and seeing the *can* rather than the *should*. And the ocean . . . " He trailed off dreamily.

"So the ocean is amoral?" Chris asked.

"Aye," the professor agreed, which meant he was getting both philosophical and dramatic. "Amoral and quixotic. Beautiful, I would say, but also deadly. It's that dichotomy that has always drawn me."

"Oh-*kay* . . . " Chris tried. He had a sudden need for a dictionary. Professor Griffin smiled.

"Chris, I *am* sorry. You don't really want to listen to an old man wax poetic about the second true love I ever had, do you?"

"I guess I don't feel quite the same way about the ocean that you do," Chris said. Professor Griffin clapped him on the shoulder.

"And that's perfectly fine—I'm just feeling melancholy today. The other love of my life—well, you don't want to hear about it."

"No, go on," Chris said. The professor had always been single and had never expressed any interest in dating, and as far as Chris knew he'd never been married or anything like that. And anyway, what else was Chris going to go do, get yelled at by Carrie?

"Ah," the professor laughed, "there's not much to tell. We were . . . two schools of fish, destined to go in opposite directions around the equator for all our lives. And she's gone now, so I'll never know—it's just a shame. You make me think of things that were," he said sadly. "Back when I saw so many ways that things could go right."

"I'm . . . sorry?" Chris offered.

Professor Griffin put a hand on Chris's shoulder and stared deeply and uncomfortably into his eyes, said earnestly, "You're a good soul, Chris," and wandered off in the direction of the cabin and the radio, leaving behind a puzzled Chris.

"That was very weird," Chris finally said to himself, and decided to get to know the grad students.

This was, strangely enough, much easier said than done. Brad was stretched out on the deck napping when Chris tracked him down, while Harvey was fiddling with the camera and grumbling about lighting.

They greeted Chris agreeably enough, and Brad welcomed him to pull up a chair—"Or a bit of deck, if you know what I mean." But when Chris started asking them questions about their research—normally an easy way to get a graduate student talking—they both clammed up. Brad kept trying to redirect the conversation to fishing, and Harvey simply mumbled and continued poking at his camera.

To be fair, coastal erosion sounded to Chris like the most agonizingly boring subject anyone could ever decide to study. But in his experience, even if a particular grad student was studying the chemistry of sand they would either talk your ear off about everything they were doing with the sand in horrifying detail, or they would declare that they never wanted to see a grain of sand again in their entire lives and then talk your ear off about *why,* the end result being the exact same horrifying amount of detail on sand chemistry. Did Brad and Harvey really study coastal erosion?

Chris squashed his question furiously, hopefully

before he made an alarmed face, and then threw himself into a conversation about fishing. Brad, at least, really was an expert. He toyed with the idea of throwing incorrect facts about coastal erosion into the conversation to test Brad or Harvey's knowledge, but then he remembered that he didn't know enough about coastal erosion to do that. And that what worked in old spy movies did not necessarily work in real life, especially not when it was almost impossible to sneak facts about coastal erosion into a discussion of fishing. Although Brad and Harvey, being grad students studying coastal erosion, could probably have managed it, but then there would be no need for the test at all.

Carrie had not moved the furniture away from the door by the time Chris fought himself free from a discussion of fly-fishing with Brad and Harvey, so he was forced to stand in the hallway and pound on the door until she cracked it open.

"What?" Carrie demanded. "I'm not letting you in if you're just going to pester me."

"I don't pester you," Chris protested. "I *was* leaving you alone, but I need to ask you a question."

Carrie groaned and dragged the door open. Chris inched inside around the desk she'd used to wedge the door shut and then replaced it as carefully as possible. Carrie stared at him. She had yellow highlighter smudged all over her fingers.

"Have you had a chance to talk to Harvey and Brad?" Chris asked when the door was shut.

"Have you seen me out of this room since we got on the boat?" Carrie asked.

"Lunch," Chris offered. "And then, uh . . . no?"

"So, unless I was talking to them through the door," Carrie said, "I haven't had a chance to." Her eyebrows were raised. This was not going to be fun.

"Okay, well I *have* had a chance to talk to them, and I think—"

"They're really impostors and they don't actually know anything about coastal erosion?"

"Yeah, actually, *how* did you come up with that?"

"They didn't try to talk my ear off about coastal erosion over lunch," Carrie said grimly. "They're probably after the map I'm making."

"Really?" Chris asked, less surprised at the idea than at the fact that Carrie had jumped to it so quickly.

"Chris, what *else* could it be? A secret embezzling ring? Illegal trade in plastic dolphin keychains? A doomed quest to prove that mermaids exist?"

"You have no faith in my detective abilities," Chris complained.

"It's the law of averages," Carrie said, flattening a book open and rummaging around behind her for a pen. "We are looking for the *San Telmo*, and you have a tendency to see suspicious persons around every corner—and I agree," she added when Chris opened his mouth to protest that he wasn't seeing things, "Brad and Harvey are a little suspicious. Actually this whole thing is a little suspicious—if you're right, then they probably picked coastal erosion on purpose because it's a perfect excuse for bringing us along."

"Because then they *have* to hug the same coastline we need to search the whole time," Chris groaned. That thought hadn't even occurred to him. Then again, Carrie thought coastal erosion was sort of interesting and knew a little about the subject. Maybe he could get *her* to drop false information into a conversation and see if they took the bait?

"Whatever you're planning, the answer is no," Carrie said.

"Not even if we could prove that Brad and Harvey are fakes in front of Professor Griffin?" Chris asked. Carrie bit her lip. Her fingers went to the neck of her shirt and then dropped; she'd been developing a nervous habit of fiddling with her locket but she'd left the locket at home.

"I'm not sure that's such a good idea," she said.

"Yeah, we have no idea what they're willing to do

if cornered," Chris agreed, but Carrie was still shaking her head.

"No, Chris—well, yes." She bit her lip. "I think Professor Griffin might suspect them already," she admitted finally.

"What? Why?"

"He's been even stranger than normal recently," Carrie said. She looked miserable. "He's more manic than usual, he's almost *too* interested in what we've been doing, and he put this trip together so fast—"

"He already had this trip planned," Chris pointed out. "Brad and Harvey told him they needed to get this done before the start of their summer TA positions." Although if Brad and Harvey weren't real grad students then that explanation fell apart. And if that explanation fell apart even for Chris and Carrie, how would Brad and Harvey have fooled Professor Griffin?

"But how could he not realize that Brad and Harvey aren't who they say they are?" Carrie asked, voicing what Chris was wondering. "Professor Griffin has had coastal-erosion students before!"

"I don't know," Chris admitted. He hadn't even known that the professor had had coastal-erosion students before.

"Maybe that's why he's letting them get away with it," Carrie suggested. "He knows that they're fake but he doesn't want to tip them off, so he's biding his time?"

"For what?"

"I don't know," Carrie admitted. "I just know that Professor Griffin is worried about something he's not telling us about."

Which would make him the second—no, the *third* person worried about something they weren't telling Chris or Carrie about. Chris still didn't know why Maddison had given him a warning tied into her hair ribbon, and then there was the undeniable fact that she'd picked up on some sort of worry from her father, whose sudden decision to drag his family halfway across the country was more than a little suspicious.

"Okay," Chris said, the letters CQD resting

uncomfortably in the forefront of his mind. "So, what do we do? Nothing?"

"Even with the professor we're nearly outnumbered," Carrie pointed out, which, wow, Chris had not even considered that yet but they really were. "And I hate to say it but this might *still* be our best chance to find the *San Telmo.* So I'm going to stay right here with the door closed and finish working out this map."

"Right," Chris said. "I'll go act casual. Don't answer the door to anyone but me," he added as a thought struck him. "I'll—I'll knock 'shave and a haircut' on the door when I come back." It was better than talking through the door, and this way Carrie didn't even have to worry about remembering the code phrases.

"Or I could just throw myself overboard," he heard Carrie mutter behind the door. "It might be less silly."

"You remember how I told you that the *San Telmo* isn't actually a cursed ship?" Robin Redd asked Bethy. It was not completely out of the blue. He'd given up on the idea of calling any of the kids from the Annie Six-Fingers shoot after Bethy demanded to know what he was planning on telling them and realized he had no answer, but he'd been noticeably subdued since the FBI agent's visit, and kept looking over his shoulder. Bethy had been forced to chase everyone onto the boat herself before Redd had snapped out of it and thrown himself into the final preparations with enthusiasm.

He was now helping Bethy stuff the much-abused card table into Bethy's equally abused car. Only two of the table's legs had consented to fold the way they were supposed to, so it was rough going, and Bethy had to quickly brace a table leg before answering.

"Please tell me you did not agree to do a show about that ship without telling me," she said. "I had to lie through my teeth to get the network off our backs when you refused the first time!"

"Hey, whoa, no!" Redd said. He did something to the backseat of Bethy's car that made the seats collapse in a way she'd never seen before, and stood back in satisfaction as the table fell into the suddenly available space. It squashed the donut Bethy had been hiding from inquisitive camera operators. Bethy poked her head in the door to try and get it out, but one of the table legs was in the way. "I just figured I should let you know," Redd explained. "It was said to have sunk along the coast of Archer's Grove. And since we're sticking to shallow water to look for manatees, I figured I should warn you. Of the possibility."

"Of sudden and unexpected treasure ships?" Bethy asked, giving up on the donut and extracting her bag instead. She was not looking forward to spending several days on a boat with Redd and the camera crew. The danger of cameras falling into the water made everyone touchy, the confined spaces meant people started picking fights, and the ship itself was barely seaworthy.

Technically it was a ship belonging to a cousin

of Flo, who *insisted* it was seaworthy. Redd thought it was perfect because it was called the *Meandering Manatee,* and Bethy had not been able to reject it because they couldn't afford anything else. That did not mean that the strings of Christmas lights decorating the cabin or the nauseating purple-and-red paint job filled her with confidence. Redd bringing up the *San Telmo* yet again filled her with even less confidence.

"Or of the treasure ship actually being haunted," Bethy continued. What was bothering Redd?

"I used to think it was haunted," Redd admitted guiltily. "Spent forever looking for the ghost stories I just knew had to be out there about the blood-soaked decks and the writhing octopus at the prow of the ship, before I realized they'd be pointless." He actually wrung his hands. Bethy folded her arms and decided to wait him out.

"There are no curses associated with the *San Telmo,*" Redd said finally. "It's never appeared as a ghost ship, and it's only interesting and mysterious because it's still missing. But if you look at the history of the people who go *looking* for the *San Telmo,* instead of the history of the ship itself, you'll notice that terrible things did—do happen around that ship. And," he added hurriedly, "there is a distinct possibility of some sort of tragedy on the high seas in the very near future, especially if there's anyone out there right now looking for the *San Telmo."*

"Because it *isn't* haunted?" Bethy asked. Redd was almost talking in code and he seemed more worried about the fact that the ship was back in the public consciousness than about it turning up as a ghost.

"Because it doesn't need to be," Redd explained, so direct and so honest that he gave Bethy chills. "There are things out there—like greed, and jealousy, and suspicion—that are much worse than ghosts."

CHAPTER
SIX

EITHER MADDISON WAS AVOIDING HER DAD OR HER dad was avoiding Maddison or they were both trying to avoid each other. Maddison was too irritated and worried to tell. But she kept walking into rooms only a step ahead of her dad, and leaving as soon as he walked into rooms, and her mother was starting to get the grim set to her mouth that said she was going to snap at one of them for being an idiot soon.

Maddison knew that spending the whole day dialing her friends' phones at regular intervals and simmering with worry when they *kept going to voicemail* was several levels of rude, especially if you were staying at someone else's house. She just couldn't stop herself. She'd barley managed to stop herself from calling both sets of Kingsolver parents multiple times, and had settled instead for calling each house twice, once to find out that Chris and Carrie were both out with Professor Griffin and wouldn't be back for at least a day, and then once a little later to ask Carrie's mom and Chris's mom if they would please tell Chris and Carrie to call her back as soon as possible.

Not that she expected them to call her. Maddison's luck was generally horrible and she expected to spend the rest of the week glued to the phone wishing someone would call her, and getting nothing. She'd even tried calling Chris and Carrie with her cell phone from the attic, but although she got a full five bars if she stood on top of the old dresser, she still couldn't get through to Chris or Carrie. The phone wasn't even ringing before going to voicemail. Maddison was stuck feeling horribly guilty for having her phone out at the dinner table, feeling terrible for spending all her time on the Lyndons' home phone in between playing cards with Mrs. Lyndon.

When Mrs. Lyndon won War and then three games of Go Fish, Maddison realized she wasn't paying enough attention to what she was doing, and surrendered the deck of cards so Mrs. Lyndon could play Solitaire. Then her cell phone finally, actually rang.

It was an unknown number, but Maddison answered with shaking hands anyway.

"Hello?" *Please, please, please don't be a telemarketer.*

"Hi! Maddison, right?" The voice was familiar, but it wasn't the familiar voice Maddison had been hoping for.

"Father Michaels?" Maddison asked in surprise.

"Yes," the priest agreed. "We met when you came by to ask me some questions about the old parish register." They had actually met when Maddison, Chris, and Carrie had fallen into the cistern in the church basement while sneaking around where they weren't supposed to and had unearthed a dead body, but

Father Michaels had ended the day by giving them tea and telling them about the parish register and was surprisingly forgiving. Maddison had no idea why he might be calling her.

"Is there . . . something wrong with the parish register?" Maddison asked weakly.

"You're the first person who picked up the phone," Father Michaels explained, which didn't really explain anything. "Maddison, this may seem completely out of line, but I'd prefer you be angry at me than in some sort of trouble. I had a man come to my door yesterday pretending to be a federal agent and asking questions about you and the parish registers."

"What?" Maddison said. "*Me*?" Had they decided to go after her father already?

"Actually, you and both your friends," Father Michaels explained. "He asked me a lot of strange questions about who had asked to see the parish registers in the past month. I called the FBI and they're looking for this phony agent but I wanted to make sure that you knew what was going on and to be careful. I really didn't like the looks of him."

For a moment, Maddison couldn't find her voice, and then when she did, the first thing she asked was, "Did you tell my dad?"

"His phone line is busy, that's why I called you."

"Of course it is," Maddison said, and thanked the priest on autopilot so she could hang up and figure out where her dad was.

He was in the study, on the phone, and Maddison heard him before she saw him, and then decided to listen in because he was arguing with someone about stalking. Specifically, that he had not noticed anyone stalking him and so this was a new development.

"Yes, well, I can hardly do anything if I don't know what the man looks like," he was saying. Maddison cautiously pushed the door open. Her dad was pacing back and forth across the small room waving one hand and scowling. "What—no! Why would I have robbed a bank?"

Maddison started edging her way into the room,

careful not to startle him. If her dad didn't know she was there he might say more than he usually did around her.

"Helen, I know you have a lot to do, I'm just saying this is turning into a matter of life and death and if I don't know what he looks like I can't—" He looked up and right at Maddison. Maddison froze. A look of supreme horror danced across her dad's face.

"Helen, I need to call you back," he said, lowering the phone from his ear and ending the call even as the person on the other end started yelling furiously.

"A matter of life and death?" Maddison asked, coming into the room and shutting the door. She wasn't seeing red, but she *was* having trouble focusing she was suddenly so angry. "When were you planning to tell *me* about this?"

"Maddison," her dad started to say.

"Don't 'Maddison' me!" On some faraway level Maddison knew that starting a fight right now was a bad idea. On the much more immediate level of right now she did not care. She had passed her tolerance level for this frustrating evasion about three weeks ago, and if her dad tried the "I'll explain everything, just not right now" route she might explode.

"I'm *telling* you . . . " Her dad was trying to stuff his phone in his pocket and failing. "This is not something you want to get involved in—"

"Yes, I can tell, you sulked around in corners spying on my friends rather than facing it!" Maddison snapped. "You *ran away to Nebraska* rather than facing it!"

"Because it almost destroyed me last time!" her dad yelled. "I *can't* watch the same thing happen to you! I *won't* let you get involved in this!"

"But, you can't seem to comprehend the fact that I am *already involved*!" Maddison yelled right back, startling both her father and herself. The windows may have rattled a little bit. They were both shaking. The chicken that had been perched in the window box directly outside the study window was upset and clucking furiously.

And then the door positively slammed open, and

Mr. Lyndon was framed in the doorway, expression somewhere between murderous and exasperated. Apparently he had heard them yelling, and apparently Mr. Lyndon had had enough.

"All right," he declared, glaring at Maddison, her father, and the chicken that was now pecking inquisitively at the glass of the window. "Both of you, sit down, now." He opened the window and said kindly to the chicken, "You shoo." Then he gave it a gentle shove out of the flower box. The chicken tried to peck at his fingers and then fluttered away in a huff. "I *mean* it," he said to Maddison and her dad, who looked at each other, and then at Mr. Lyndon, and then sat down on either end of the desk. Mr. Lyndon glared at the both of them and sighed.

"You know," he said, "I'm retired." He crossed his arms and looked up at the ceiling, as if just rolling his eyes heavenward was no longer enough. "Do you know what that means? It means I'm supposed to be done with taking witness statements forever. I'm supposed to be done with interviewing witnesses who are confused and upset, and I'm not supposed to be comparing multiple accounts of the night in question to see if there's anything they can agree on. But then, that's always been a particular problem with this case, hasn't it?"

"Greg," Maddison's dad started to say.

"Go on. You were going to explain to me why the *San Telmo* is suddenly a major factor in this case, since not once in the whole investigation did anyone other than Wyzowski mention a sunken treasure ship."

"It—it wasn't—as far as I knew, it had nothing to do with Ryan disappearing," Maddison's dad stammered, and Mr. Lyndon put his head in his hands.

"No, I mean it," Maddison's dad said, hopping off the desk so he could gesture wildly. "Greg—look, we were all friends! Wyzowski and Ryan and Griffin and I were in the same dorm off and on, we had something like six classes together—and we spent *part* of our free time looking for clues to the *San Telmo* together. But the night Ryan disappeared he told me he was going to a concert. And there'd been—tension between the five of us for a couple of weeks, so he'd been tiptoeing around me. I didn't see how Ryan's disappearance could have anything to do with the *San Telmo*, so, no, I didn't mention it."

"Wyzowski did," Mr. Lyndon said. "Wyzowski, in between telling me that there might have been alien involvement and insisting that he had never once in his entire life tried any kind of mood-altering substance, told me that Ryan Moore had been really excited because he had just found a new clue to the mystery of the lost treasure of the *San Telmo*. He said Ryan was going to meet you to go looking for it the night he disappeared."

"What?"

"Wait," Maddison said. "Who was the fifth person?" Her dad and Mr. Lyndon turned to stare at her, her dad opening his mouth uncertainly. Mr. Lyndon looked proud that she'd noticed. "You said you and Ryan and Wyzowski and Griffin, but that's only four. Who else was there?"

"I . . . " her dad said.

"Kevin," Mr. Lyndon said. He sounded irritated. "You're going to have to tell her eventually. I'm honestly shocked that you've managed this far without needing to explain."

"Explain *what*?" Maddison wailed.

Her dad sighed. "It wasn't just me and Ryan and Griffin and Wyzowski," he explained. "There was another person, one who never deserved any of this."

"And?" Maddison asked impatiently.

"She didn't share a dorm room with us, obviously," her dad said. "They wouldn't do co-ed dorms for another three years."

"*Who*?" Maddison demanded. Her dad sat down heavily in Mr. Lyndon's desk chair and grabbed a random pen so he didn't have to look at anyone.

"Elsie Kingsolver," he said.

CHAPTER
SEVEN

"We were all in the same geography class our freshman year," Maddison's dad explained. Maddison was staring at him and there was a weird rushing noise in her ears. Hopefully it wasn't shock, if she passed out now it would be embarrassing. That, and her dad would probably try to explain how he knew Chris and Carrie's Aunt Elsie while Maddison was out cold so he never actually had to tell her anything.

"I was assigned to room with Ryan, and we'd met Griffin at orientation, and he had a math class with Elsie, and then Ryan made friends with Wyzowski and just turned up with him one day, and nobody ever knew where they met," Maddison's dad explained, waving a hand as if to indicate that that part wasn't important.

"The tables in the geography lecture hall seated five comfortably—they were supposed to be able to seat six—and the rest is history," he went on. "We were inseparable for the next three-and-a-half years. We were planning to go into fields that were . . . I guess you might say . . . complementary? History, geology, archives, and oceanography all play into each other, especially if you spend your free time treasure hunting. And Elsie was—kind of terrifying," her dad said. "She had the most incredible mind. She loved puzzles and she'd practiced all kinds until she could look at a collection of separate objects and tell you three different ways you could fit them together. She was the one who started the whole search for the *San Telmo*," he explained. "It was this little sidebar in our geography textbooks and I'd been interested in the history behind it. We were sitting over lunch talking about it one day and suddenly Elsie said, 'Well, why hasn't anyone ever looked into the lee side of Archer's Grove?' and all of a sudden the theory became practice." He had a faraway look in his eyes. Maddison was afraid to breathe too loudly for fear she'd break the spell.

Chris and Carrie hadn't talked about their aunt that much. They had both known her all their lives, so Maddison supposed that there was little for them to discuss, and the loss was still too fresh for either of Maddison's friends to feel like sharing. Maddison had known that Elsie Kingsolver was a much-loved woman, but she'd always been a plot point rather than a character in her own right. And now she turned out to have been a major player in Maddison's family history, too.

"Sometimes, I think Elsie saw how the five of us fit together better than anyone else," Maddison's dad added. He picked up a snow globe from Mr. Lyndon's desk and turned it over. "And then, Ryan went missing and suddenly none of my other friends would talk to me," he said, watching the white flakes swirl around. "And the police were asking me all these leading questions and only the police chief overseeing the case seemed to think I was telling the truth when I said I hadn't done anything."

"Except act like an idiot teenager," Mr. Lyndon said.

"Well, what was I supposed to do, develop psychic abilities and report Ryan missing before he left?"

"Mention the *San Telmo* before today?"

"There was *nothing* to connect the *San Telmo* with Ryan disappearing!" Maddison's dad protested. "And there had been arguments between all of us the week before, it was right before finals and we were . . . hormonal."

"What does *that* mean?" Maddison asked, and then got a very good idea when her dad covered his face with his hands and blushed. Mr. Lyndon raised an amused eyebrow.

"Elsie had started dating a guy and I didn't like him," her dad admitted.

"Did you like *her*?" Maddison asked. "What?" she added when her dad looked horrified. "It's an important question, lovers' spats are practically the first thing they check for when someone goes missing!"

"Valid point," Mr. Lyndon said. Maddison preened.

"I actually didn't," Maddison's dad said. "We were really good friends for a really long time, and we both thought about it, but in the end—I saw fireworks when I met your mother. I was never in love with Elsie Kingsolver in the same way."

"But you still dragged us to her funeral," Maddison said. "Without explaining anything to me or—actually, did you ever tell Mom this?"

"I had to tell your mom, she wanted to know why I was so interested in taking her name when we got married," her dad explained. "I very nearly didn't get into any graduate program at all because of Ryan's disappearance. My grades suffered and I had to explain to every school where I interviewed why I was the subject of an ongoing police investigation—and yes," he said to Mr. Lyndon, "I know that you did everything you could to stop that and that it wasn't legal for the schools to be getting letters about me, but that didn't matter to the vultures. I was getting anonymous phone calls too. A bunch of people thought I did something to Ryan."

"I never understood that," Mr. Lyndon added. "There was no more evidence that you did it than there was that the Wyzowski kid did it, but for some reason everyone assumed we were going to arrest you. I even had to have words with a couple of the local cops on the subject of blabbing to reporters."

"Anyway," Maddison's dad said hurriedly, "I had a heck of a time moving on from the whole mess, and when I met your mother in our first year of graduate school I told her before our first date. She's always known."

Maddison sighed.

"I was trying to put the whole thing in the past," her dad said. "The last thing I wanted was for someone to make your life a nightmare because they remembered my part in a disappearance years ago. So, I didn't tell you, and I didn't see anyone from school for eighteen years, and as far as we were all concerned it was over. Nobody even contacted me, except for one letter from Elsie right after you were born, wishing me luck. And then . . . " He paused. "Then Elsie sent me a letter. A postcard, really. It had a picture of a Spanish galleon on the front and 'It's starting again' written on the back in an old keyword cypher we used to use." Maddison gasped. "And two days later I found out," her dad said, "that she was dead."

"Was her name the key?" Maddison asked.

"That was her favorite," her dad agreed. "And then . . . well you know the rest . . . "

Maddison did, sort of. Her dad's story explained so much—the paranoia, the insistence on going to the funeral, the moving across the state and taking a new job at the drop of a hat, the weird avoidance of Professor Griffin, even the stalking of Chris and Carrie. It just also all seemed so pointless.

"You know, we wasted a heck of a lot of time in the beginning, wondering if you were out to kill everybody," Maddison said, and her dad choked. "No, really," Maddison said, warming to her subject. "You kept following Chris and Carrie around and being creepily nosey! I had a screaming fight with Chris because he was absolutely convinced you were going to murder him in his sleep and I *still* don't think he trusts you at all. And what was the deal with following Carrie around and taking pictures of her?"

"Wait, what?" Her dad looked now more confused than guilty, which Maddison felt was an annoying response to a legitimate complaint.

"Taking pictures of your teenage daughter's friends without asking either girl for permission *is* a very suspicious thing to do, Kevin," Mr. Lyndon added.

"I agree," Maddison's dad said, looking puzzled. "But I haven't actually done anything like that."

Oh, this was ridiculous. "I saw the picture," Maddison said. "It fell out of one of your folders in the study when I was trying to find your glasses."

Her dad continued to look bewildered. "Here, look," Maddison said, and pulled the picture of the picture up on her phone. "See?"

"Oh," her dad said. "That's not—Maddison, that isn't a picture of Carrie."

Maddison looked from her dad to the picture and back again, letting her incredulity show on her face.

"Has anybody ever mentioned to Carrie how very much she looks like her aunt did at that age?" Maddison's dad asked in a slightly strained voice.

"This is Elsie?" Maddison asked.

"Carrie *really* looks like her aunt," her dad said.

✗ ✗ ✗

"The Kingsolver case?" Detective Hermann said. "Yeah, what about it?" He'd been about to head home. It was six o'clock and the police station was switching over to night shift, and Detective Hermann had been hard at work since seven in the morning with exactly one break, during which someone had accidentally walked off with his chips. He'd tracked them down to Detective Barrie, who hadn't even realized they were in her bag and returned them in perfect condition, but that was the biggest success Detective Hermann had had all day.

The convenience store robber had struck again, there had been another flare-up of the graffiti artist who kept bothering the park service, and no progress had been made at all in the Kingsolver case. The *murder* of Elsie Kingsolver—if, as Detective Hermann still had to convince some people, it truly was a murder—had been stuck ever since the suspiciously convenient suspect had committed a completely out-of-character suicide. So when the two federal agents came in asking for him, he was only too happy to help.

"I'm Agent Michelle Grey, this is Forrest Holland," the woman with the slightly more commanding presence said, shaking hands with the detective. Her partner shook hands and then wandered off to stand guard over the fax machine. "He's expecting DNA- and dental-record confirmation," she explained. "We're sorry to keep you through dinner, but we came by earlier today and missed you. We wanted your take on the Kingsolver case."

"I just don't see what I can tell you," Detective Hermann explained. "It was initially classified as a hit-and-run, until we caught someone trying to kill her niece and nephew. I had to call in a favor just to keep the case open when the guy committed suicide in a holding cell."

"And there's the niece and nephew again," Agent Grey sighed. "Oh, I hate being right."

CHAPTER
EIGHT

PUTTING TOGETHER TWO WRITTEN DESCRIPTIONS and three maps from vastly different time periods in just the right order was tricky. Doing so in just the right way so they overlapped and gave you the fabled location of a sunken ship was not an exact science. If Carrie were a professional cartographer it might be, but Carrie was not a professional cartographer and so they were all going to have to be happy with what she could manage. She'd found the part of the island that had mussel beds and compared that to the part of the island someone could reasonably see from the old mission church. Then she had matched that area to the only place on the island that had ever been described as having white cliffs. They weren't visible as cliffs anymore, which had been a huge part of the problem of getting the location right; at some point in the fifties the area had been developed and then torn down and then planted over with hardy grasses, and what had been a cliff that gave way abruptly to a stretch of marshy land that led out into the ocean was now a seldom-used beach.

Such was the march of time. But what was important was this: Carrie had narrowed the number of places Father Gonzalez could have been describing in his account to three, all in the same area no more than a couple of miles across. She had, after careful thought, picked a point in the exact center of the area and arbitrarily declared that that was the point they needed to find. Then she'd looked that point up on an actual map, instead of the colored one in *Endangered Floridian Mollusks* or one of the ones she'd printed off and scribbled all over. It was right in the middle of nowhere, and also near the legendary screaming caves of Archer's Grove, but hopefully the actual shipwreck would not be smack in the middle of the supposedly haunted and/or cursed caves that lay along a deserted sandy shoreline in a remote part of the island.

"Okay," Carrie said to herself, checking that she had the correct sticky note with the correct coordinates written on it in her hand. "Time to go see how serious Professor Griffin is about finding this ship."

She didn't entirely want to. There was something up with Professor Griffin, and Carrie wasn't sure what it was. All she was sure about was that the professor was preoccupied and worried about something. He could be afraid, he could be convinced the *San Telmo* was a fake and was just humoring them, he could have finally gone completely around the bend and decided to go looking for white whales, she just didn't know. And the not knowing was slowly driving her crazy. If nothing else, the professor's actions had been out of character ever since he had brought up the FBI and asked Carrie and Chris if they knew where Maddison and her family were, and Carrie couldn't shake the feeling that there was something more to that. Why would the professor bother to notice the FBI investigating, even if they had talked to him?

Carrie found Professor Griffin in the main cabin, singing to himself about anchors away and sketching the sun in colored pencil. He had his feet up on the dashboard and was swiveling back and forth in his chair.

"Hey," she said, and he jumped, almost guiltily.

"Carrie! You've been noticeably absent all day, everything all right?"

"I was just finishing things up," Carrie said honestly. It was edging toward night outside and the sun was setting gloriously below the horizon, painting the sky purple and red. It was probably why Professor Griffin had his sketchpad out. The sticky note in her pocket was sticking to her palm.

"The final resting place of the *San Telmo*," she said, holding it out.

"Ah! Really?" Professor Griffin plucked the note

out of Carrie's hand and squinted at it. "Glasses would be a good idea," he added, fishing them out of his shirt pocket.

"It's hardly exact," Carrie pointed out, watching the professor as he leaned across the console and made a couple of careful adjustments to the direction they were heading. "I picked a point in the middle of the likeliest-looking spot."

"Close only ever counts with horseshoes and hand grenades," Professor Griffin said, tucking the sticky note in his pocket.

"Um, Professor?"

"That sounded a good deal better in my head," Professor Griffin admitted after thinking it through. "I think it means something different than what I was intending—what I *meant* to say, Carrie, my dear, was that somewhere in the middle is good enough for me."

"That makes a little more sense," Carrie agreed, edging toward the door. "I'm going to go tell Chris we have a new heading, maybe he'll stop pestering the grad students about coastal erosion."

"Ah," Professor Griffin said, turning back to the sunset. "Let him pester them! I've never known a grad student who didn't secretly want to spend their entire evening talking your ear off about their subject matter."

More like, let him pester them, Carrie thought, *since he can't get anything out of them, since I doubt they're real grad students.* The faint unease she had felt all day was suddenly a lump of lead in her stomach as she went directly to the room she and Chris were sharing and started packing all her books and papers into her duffle bag.

Apparently, knowing in theory how to sail was finally coming in handy, because apparently Professor Griffin did *not* know that Carrie could figure out which direction a person was steering a boat. At least, she knew quite well that the adjustments the professor had made to their course as soon as she showed him the sticky note had taken them *away* from the coast and not toward it. She'd been wondering if there was something bothering the professor; she now had a terrible feeling it was a guilty conscience, because he was clearly lying about something. If she'd wanted an answer to whether the professor was hiding something she now had one, it just happened to be exactly the sort of answer she didn't want.

Carrie paused in the middle of wrestling a map back into its original folded shape and abruptly decided that she needed evidence stored in more than one place. Most of the books and papers she had with her were more reference material than anything else, so if anyone looked through them they wouldn't be able to re-create Carrie's research. But the map she'd done all her work on would point someone in exactly the right direction. Carrie hauled her duffle bag back onto her bunk and yanked it open, digging out the map in question and fumbling her phone out of her jeans pocket as she did. She still didn't get any service, but her phone could take pictures, so she saved a version of the map on her phone and stuffed the original copy in her pocket. Then it occurred to Carrie that pictures on her phone were only as safe as her phone was, and her phone was a small plastic rectangle surrounded by gallons upon gallons of seawater. True, she had a waterproof case, but she'd never actually tested it beyond using the phone in the rain.

So, evidence cleared away and map documented in two different formats, Carrie went in search of Chris and a plastic bag to put her phone in.

Chris had been poking around *Moby* and was now nosing around a corner of the equipment room. Carrie stopped in the doorway and rapped "shave and a haircut" on the doorframe, causing him to bang his head on a shelf in the process of looking up.

"Um," Carrie said, mildly embarrassed she was even considering doing this, "excuse me while I go to the restroom briefly." Then she left to do a circuit of the ship in search of a plastic bag before Chris could respond. But Chris was the one who'd come up with both "shave and a haircut" and "Excuse me while I go to the restroom briefly" as a signal, so if he didn't realize she was trying to warn him, Carrie was going to be very annoyed.

Aside from the equipment room—which housed cables, a first aid kit, other stuff for tending to *Moby* and its operators and thus needed to be well lit "so we can see if there's blood," as Abigail tended to put it—the *Triangle* was dimly lit for such a small ship. The professor had always attributed it to an unfortunate accident involving a string of pineapple-shaped Christmas tree lights and a blown fuse, but it could simply be that the ship was older or that the professor used the wrong kind of light bulbs. Either way it was difficult to find a plastic bag in the gathering dusk on a ship that was increasingly full of dark corners, and it took Carrie an embarrassingly long time to remember that she had a plastic bag full of hairbands in the bathroom.

The hairbands were, of course, sitting obviously on the lip of the tiny bathroom sink, impersonating a bag of spiders. Carrie fished one hairband out and absent-mindedly snapped it around her wrist, dumped the rest of them in her palm, and slid her phone into the empty bag. It was a freezer bag, so the phone fit, but then she had to spend a whole minute squeezing the air out of the bag before she could get it to zip, and then the resulting bundle of plastic and phone didn't want to fit in her pocket.

She was stuffing the phone *down* in her pocket and muttering about useless pockets when she pushed the bathroom door open and ran directly into one of the grad students—it was the nervous-looking one, Harvey—who was hovering right in front of the door.

"Hi?" Carrie said, hairbands scattering everywhere. She gathered them up and tried to edge around him towards the equipment room and hopefully Chris. But Harvey wouldn't let her push past him. "Um," Carrie said, stomach sinking in realization even as the rational part of her mind tried to say there was a perfectly innocent explanation for all this. "I'm sorry if you needed to pee, I was just getting my stuff out of the bathroom so it's free!"

Real smooth, Carrie thought, horrified at her own

babbling. It had even *rhymed*. If she'd had any hope of convincing Professor Griffin that she didn't know what he and his—accomplices? minions? definitely not real grad students—were planning, she'd just lost it. Because at this point she really couldn't deny it any longer; whatever the fake grad students were up to, Professor Griffin was up to it with them.

"Excuse me," Carrie told Harvey, and fled in the only direction she could—out onto the deck of the ship. And, of *course*, that particular side of the ship was framed on one side by a railing and on the other by a crane arm that was supposed to be for *Moby* but hadn't been able to lift the submersible since the camera had been added. And the door to below-decks didn't exactly lock, although Carrie slammed it closed hard enough to get someone right in the nose before it bounced back open and Harvey followed her through.

"Okay, look," Harvey said, cautiously edging toward Carrie, who backed up to keep the same amount of space between them. Brad was swearing viciously and somewhat thickly behind Harvey, clutching his bleeding nose. Carrie refused to feel guilty, and anyway, where had he even come from?

"I know this looks really bad," Harvey said. He looked incredibly nervous and deeply uncomfortable and Carrie figured that was only fair. "But I promise, I didn't mean to scare you, it was just a misunderstanding, don't do anything rash—"

Carrie backed into the boat's railing and couldn't go any farther unless she wanted to try walking on water.

"Okay, I'm going to take a step back . . . " Harvey said, and then yelped when Brad staggered to his feet and shoved Harvey aside.

"Wha' the hell do you tink you're doing?" he demanded. "We were paid to do a dob!"

"We can't just—" Harvey protested, grabbing ineffectually at Brad, who was coming at Carrie with murder in his eyes (on second thought, breaking his nose had maybe not been the best move).

"Get ob me!" Brad roared, and lunged at Carrie, who couldn't exactly move out of the way, and only missed her by virtue of Harvey making a swipe at his arm. Carrie ducked a tangle of flailing limbs, and then someone screamed in pain (it wasn't her) and she narrowly avoided getting punched in the stomach. Brad *did* manage to grab her by the legs and heft her up. Carrie stabbed him as hard as she could in the eye, and there was another scream, and then she went up . . .

. . . and over the railing.

She managed to grab a breath before she hit the water with a painful splash, but most of the air was still knocked out of her lungs and cold seawater went up her nose. She broke the surface coughing and gasping, blinking water desperately out of her eyes and treading water for dear life.

Chris would maintain until the end of time itself that it wasn't that he didn't register Carrie using his own distress code to warn him, it was that he was in the middle of a terrible realization of his own. Two terrible realizations of his own, actually.

First: *Moby* was missing its camera and the laptop that went with it—he'd thought they'd just been removed and stored in the equipment room, but a careful search had not turned them up. Without the waterproof camera hooked up to the little submersible, it was impossible for *Moby* to record any footage from the seafloor. And without the laptop that Abigail had painstakingly programmed to hook up to *Moby*'s camera, it was impossible to see what *Moby* was doing on the seafloor in real time. True, *Moby*'s robot arm looked to be in working order so the little guy could still take samples from the ocean floor, but the stated mission of the current expedition, at least according to Harvey, was to take pictures of the coastline above and below the water, and for that *Moby* was currently useless. It would be a pretty terrible result if two grad students made special arrangements to do research and then weren't able to *do* half of the research; at the very least Brad and Harvey should have discovered the missing hardware within the first five minutes of setting sail and turned the whole expedition around to get it. They should have chased Abigail and the van halfway across the island in order to get the equipment they needed.

Unless, of course, the camera wasn't attached to *Moby* because the trip was a decoy. The camera and the laptop were the newest and most expensive pieces of equipment that weren't attached directly to *Moby*, so if someone wanted to make sure the delicate and expensive equipment wasn't in any danger, it made sense to leave them both behind. Chris did not like what that said about how the trip might end.

Then, Chris rummaged around in the toolbox, trying to figure out why the submersible was missing its camera—and found a small gray box amongst the screws. He only recognized it as a cell phone jammer because he'd seen one before. Aunt Elsie had brought one home from work when the board voted to put cell phone jammers in the archive reading room to cut down on people trying to smuggle cell phones into the room, then discovered how unpopular an idea it was and nixed the project, but not before buying two of the devices. Aunt Elsie had sighed and taken one home, giving one to the English professor at the college.

But there was really only one explanation for a cell phone jammer hidden in the toolbox of *The Vanishing Triangle*. Chris turned the box over until he found a likely looking switch and flipped it, and then checked his cell phone and discovered he had three bars.

He'd been breathing hard and there had been blood pounding in his ears—it was flat-out scary being stuck on a boat with someone who wanted to cut off communication with the outside world—and so it was only when he had rehidden the jammer in the can of screws that he realized something was happening above decks. There was a storm of swearing going on in the background and Chris poked his head out of the equipment room to see what the matter was and who had splintered the bathroom door. Then he remembered what Carrie had said while he was looking for *Moby's* camera, and decided to follow the commotion to its source.

The swearing sounded like Brad and wasn't hard to follow, but Chris was only two steps up to the deck when he heard a yell and a scream and a splash, and *that* was when he started running.

Everyone else was standing on the deck when he shot through the door and skidded to a stop next to the lifeboat. Brad was doubled over and bleeding from his nose, Harvey had both hands clapped over his mouth in apparent horror, and the professor, clutching his hat, looked uncertain. And Carrie—Carrie *wasn't on the boat.*

"What happened?" Chris asked. Harvey shook his head.

"Chris," the professor said, "I need you to be calm and logical about all this—"

"What happened and where's Carrie?" Chris demanded, and Harvey pointed a shaking finger over the side of the boat at a fast-receding figure in the water.

"She fell in?" Chris yelped, looking from Harvey to the professor as the two most likely to actually answer him. "Well, did anyone throw her a lifejacket?"

The professor opened his mouth and then closed it again.

"Then what are you waiting for?" Chris yelled, already grabbing two from the three that were right next to the lifeboat. Then, either because an instinct told him staying on the ship was not the best option or habit had him rushing into situations that could get him killed, he threw himself off the boat after Carrie.

She was several yards off the back of the boat, frantically trying to stay afloat in the waves and the wake of the ship. Chris used his best sidestroke while hauling the life vests to reach her and it was still a near thing.

"Are you all right?" he asked, offering her a life-jacket. The day had been hot, but night was coming on fast and the water was cold and Carrie was starting to shiver.

"I'm fine—look out!" Carrie said, her eyes growing huge.

"What—*hey*!"

The *Triangle* made a tight turn that swamped them in a wave, then steamed away at full speed.

"What the hell are you thinking! Get *back* here!" Chris yelled. "What the hell?" he added to Carrie when nobody turned back. Carrie raised an eyebrow as much as possible while also struggling into the life-jacket Chris had brought her.

"You're swearing," she said mildly.

"We just got dumped in the middle of the ocean!" Chris pointed out, on the off-chance Carrie hadn't quite noticed it.

"Gee, I hadn't noticed," Carrie grumbled, spitting out seawater. "Even though Brad threw me overboard."

"He *what*?"

"Chris, chill," Carrie said. "Save your energy. We have no idea how long we're going to be stuck here."

"That—that—oh I'm going to *kill* him!" Chris

snarled, punching the water. And to think they'd brought Professor Griffin into this because they were afraid *he* might be in danger.

"Chris!" Carrie said. "Stop thrashing around!"

Chris froze completely, remembering with sudden horrifying detail all the times they'd been told to avoid wearing shiny things or thrashing around in shallow water or looking too much like a seal for fear of sharks. Really, he knew that shark attacks were less of a danger than car crashes, but then, car crashes seemed to be a problem for people in his family. And now that the first heat of anger had passed the "should-have-dones" were occurring to Chris.

"I probably shouldn't have jumped over the side after you," Chris admitted.

"At least you remembered to grab two lifejackets before you jumped overboard," Carrie allowed. "And to be honest I'm not sure you would have been safe on board the *Triangle* anyway. At least the ocean is up-front about how dangerous it is."

CHAPTER NINE

"But what I don't understand," Maddison said to her dad, "is why Professor Griffin would want to blame you for everything."

She was pacing back and forth in Mr. Lyndon's study, her dad doing the same thing but in a different direction. She'd tried to put her dad's admission behind them, as much as possible, but she kept going back and asking questions. Talking about Elsie Kingsolver had devastated Maddison's dad, but for the first time ever he was answering all of Maddison's questions and she was desperately seizing the chance to brainstorm with him before he decided to clam up again.

And he didn't seem to mind her too much. Maddison had left the dinner table and gone off to find a quiet place to think and her dad had followed a minute later and started poring over a handful of newspaper clippings from a file folder, but then Maddison had demanded he tell her if her summary of the situation was correct and he'd abandoned his reading material to help her.

"I can understand you looking like the most likely subject to everyone," Maddison said. "You were the last person to see Ryan alive and had also argued with him recently and that would put you at the top of any suspect list."

"Gee thanks, Mads."

"But if Professor Griffin was the only person who said he saw you with Ryan, then that sounds as though he was trying to make it look like you were responsible," Maddison continued. "Which might make sense if he were trying to throw suspicion *away* from someone, but then who would he be trying to protect?" Maddison turned to her dad. "Was there anybody Professor Griffin cared about more than the rest?"

"Well," her dad said, stopping short. "Elsie? But Elsie was the only person who tried to contact me after the fact, so that could point either way, really."

"And if she was responsible for Ryan's disappearance—and if we assume that the disappearance had something to do with the *San Telmo*—then why would she warn you right before she died?"

"We're assuming Ryan's disappearance was linked to the *San Telmo*?" Maddison's dad asked.

"It's a decent intuitive leap," Mr. Lyndon offered. He had wandered in and settled in his desk chair with a glass of cider and a pleased expression, as if he were greatly enjoying Maddison and her father working in tandem and quite pleased with what he had wrought. And to be fair, he was mostly responsible. "If only we had made such a leap nineteen years ago . . . " Mr. Lyndon added.

"I get it, I get it!" Maddison's dad waved his arms in the air. "In that case, though . . . after Ryan, the person who got most into searching for the *San Telmo* was Willis."

"Really?"

"He saw it as a chance to prove himself, I think. I never really understood what he thought about the ship. He did always want to talk about what we'd do *when* we found it, instead of *if* we found it. He worked twice as hard as the rest of us digging for clues and looking for the ship in the historical record."

"So, he would care about being the one to find it?" Maddison suggested.

"Well, more than the rest of us," her dad agreed. "And we used to joke that the Florida tax on shipwrecks was so high that the fewer of us alive when we found the ship the better—oh hell."

"You don't think?" Maddison said. Mr. Lyndon sat up abruptly. "You don't think he would—would get rid of someone before they could find the *San Telmo* before him?"

"I—I never did know, with Willis."

"You knew *something*," Maddison said. "You didn't want him anywhere near me!"

"Because he has it in for me!" her dad protested. "And Willis Griffin holds long grudges!"

"Long enough for murder?" Maddison asked. "We never did figure out who was behind the guy who did those car crashes, but we know he used to work for the school through dining services. And then *someone* has always been one step behind us, especially Chris and Carrie, and they tell Professor Griffin everything because he's an old family friend! What if—what if the reason we've always been one step ahead of this person, and *only* one step ahead of them, is because they've always been right there listening at the dinner table?!"

Her dad had gone white.

"Maddison, do you know if Griffin is still out on a boat with Chris and Carrie right now?" he asked.

"No," Maddison admitted miserably, "I still can't get through to them."

"But they're just looking for some of the landmarks for the ship, right?" her dad asked, and Maddison realized that in all the confusion she had never told her father exactly what the trip on the boat was supposed to accomplish. The steps they'd taken to get to the *San Telmo* had felt, at the time, like a lot of one step forward and two steps back, with occasional falling into cisterns, and then the last bit had snuck up on them and Maddison hadn't really let it sink in that if they played it right Chris and Carrie could have found the ship on this trip.

But it probably had occurred to Professor Griffin.

"Dad," Maddison said, "Carrie was in the middle of narrowing the shipwreck sites down to three or four points in the same area. They were hoping to actually find the ship today or tomorrow."

"Oh no," her father sighed, and scrabbled around on the end table until he came up with his phone. Maddison decided this was a good time to try dialing Chris and Carrie again, and Mr. Lyndon excused himself to go do something. Possibly to call a contact in the National Guard; Mr. Lyndon was terrifyingly resourceful.

"Hi, Helen," her dad said as Maddison sat down with a phone pressed to her ear. The call went directly to voicemail and she groaned. "No, I—yes, it was very rude of me to hang up on you like that. No, I—yes, I owe you an apology. I know your time is very valuable, will you just—Helen! Yes! Oh for—you still have a brother in the Coast Guard Auxiliary, right?"

"Hi Chris, it's Maddison," Maddison said, leaving her eighteenth message of the day and not even feeling awkward about it. "I'm just trying to see where you are, call me when you get this?" She hung up. If all she could do now was wait she might explode.

"Okay, I've poked the Coast Guard Auxiliary. Helen has some pull with them," Maddison's dad said. He looked mildly confused, which he always did whenever he had to talk to Helen Kinney. "I think we should probably be back in Archer's Grove as soon as possible—" he added when Mr. Lyndon stuck his head back in the doorway.

"Already handled," Mr. Lyndon said. "Of course you need to go pack up your things *now,* the flight I booked you on leaves in two hours."

"Greg—"

"Go. Answer any and all questions to the best of your ability, try not to act too suspicious around the agents or the officers, and for the love of the blasted chickens"—there was one roosting in the window box—"visit me without a tragedy following you next time," Mr. Lyndon said.

✗ ✗ ✗

Michelle Grey was one of the few people so used to being called out of bed at all hours of the night that she didn't grumble about it. She just opened the door and caught Forrest when he fell through mid-knock.

"Please tell me it's just the confirmation on the dental matches," she said. "This is a nice, pleasant community, if there is an underground drug trade they want us to help root out I'll bet it's nasty."

"Detective Hermann said to ask the park service about that, apparently they deal with some smuggling in the national forests," Forrest told her. "It seems the mussels are sometimes in danger."

Michelle risked a glance at the digital clock and glared. Then she transferred the glare to Forrest. "I'm going to pretend I was dreaming, because otherwise I could swear you just told me the mussels are sometimes in danger."

"But more importantly they finally got the DNA and dental results confirmed," Forrest said hurriedly. "You were right. This is now a reopened and reclassified case that initially dates back to the early nineties and involved"—he stopped halfway down the page—"a lot of people from the Kingsolver case, actually. Way more than random chance, they do look connected."

"I so hate it when I'm right," Michelle said, scanning the page Forrest offered her. "Have you talked with Detective Hermann about putting any of these people in protective custody?"

"I just got off the phone with him," Forrest said, "and . . . there's a complication."

✗ ✗ ✗

"Moon's pretty," Chris offered. Carrie poked him hard in the side. They were treading water facing each other, trying very, very hard to avoid thinking about what might be out there in the water with them and how they were going to get home. They'd had a brief, furious argument about staying put or trying to swim for shore which Carrie had won by pointing out that they didn't know what direction to swim in. They were now out of conversation topics.

It was maddening, because they couldn't be that far from land. *The Vanishing Triangle* had been hugging the coastline for most of its trip and Archer's Grove had been visible from the deck the whole time, but the professor had steered the ship into open waters as soon as Carrie had given him the coordinates, and when Carrie and Chris had fallen overboard they'd lost all sense of direction. The *Triangle* could not have made it that far before they'd fallen overboard, but without knowing which direction to go Chris and Carrie couldn't risk swimming for it and sending themselves farther out to sea. Staying put looked like the best option, especially with the ocean currently so calm, and so it was the safest thing to do.

"Although I don't think the survival tips are designed for people who have purposely been thrown overboard," Chris pointed out. "The idea is to stay in one place so the ship can come back and get you, and we might not *want* the professor to find us."

Carrie had agreed, for the time being. Carrie's phone had managed to stay in her pocket even as she fell, but taking it out to see if the plastic bag had held and if they could even use it in the middle of nowhere seemed like an action that could go horribly wrong.

"Plus, if it's still working even a little bit someone might be able to find us through the signal," Carrie had added, so it stayed in her pocket.

"Well, I could talk about sharks or ghost ships," Chris told his cousin since she'd rejected his admiration of the moon. "But I don't want to scare myself."

"Chris, you cussed out the whole ocean for about fifteen minutes, there isn't a life form in shouting distance that hasn't fled by this point."

"I was angry!" Chris said. He'd been left in the ocean to drown. He had every right to be mad. "Aren't you furious?"

"Oh, yeah," Carrie said. "Three of the books in my bag were library books!"

"Carrie . . . "

"Even if we get out of this, who knows if I'll ever get them back! One was an out-of-state loan, too, they have a fifty-cent per day fine and the replacement costs are super high!"

"Are you seriously going to freak out about losing a couple of library books?" Chris asked. It was a very Carrie thing to do, but Chris had a vague feeling that panicking was a bad idea and he should definitely not let her cry. She'd lose precious fluids if she cried, and she might swallow even more seawater.

"I don't want to pay thirty dollars in library fines," Carrie wailed.

Chris was kind of at a loss. "Do you want a hug?" he offered. Carrie bit down on the tears and took a couple of deep breaths and shook her head.

"No, I'm fine. I actually should have thrown my whole bag over the side if I had the chance. If I have left even one *hint* for that jerk to find the *San Telmo* I'll never forgive myself."

"I don't think—" Chris stopped.

"You were about to say, 'I don't think the professor's going to go through your bag,' weren't you?" Carrie said. "This sucks. Go ahead and tell me about the ghost ship."

"Er." Chris had accidentally spent a night last week reading about ghost ships, but he was hardly an expert.

"I keep wondering if I've felt something nudging

my leg," Carrie explained. "I need some sort of distraction."

"Well, there are a whole lot of ghost ships," Chris said, every single fact he knew about ghost ships flying out of his head as he did. *Famous ghost ships, famous ghost ships, even just famous ships with strange things connected to them*, he thought frantically. "Well, there's the *Flying Dutchman*," he said desperately. "Cursed to sail the seas forever after the captain swore to reach his destination or die trying. There's the *Lady Lovibond*, the *Mary Celeste*, the *MV Joyita*—those two don't haunt so much as they went mysteriously missing and then turned up deserted—the *Young Teazer* . . ."

"That ship," Carrie said faintly.

"Which ship?" Chris asked. Carrie grabbed him by the shoulders and turned him around. Chris choked, and it wasn't on seawater.

It certainly did not look like a ship any sane living human would get on. The hull was two different colors, and the deck appeared to be painted with blood. There was a strange purple figure floating just above the cabin, and it was glowing.

"Do we try to flag them down?" Carrie asked.

"You see it too?" Chris asked. A silly question, since Carrie was the one who'd pointed it out to him, but he was toying with the idea of plunging under the surface and holding his breath until it sailed away.

✗ ✗ ✗

The moon had made it over the horizon, and moonlight shone off a sliver of sand and bounced amongst the tangles of vegetation all along the stretch of shoreline. It was pretty, in an entirely unromantic way, and the boat hugging the edge of the shoreline only added to the picture. This was a shame, because the two people leaning against the railing were hardly cut out for appreciating the gentle beauty of nature.

Harvey Tanner was leaning heavily against the railing, trying not to be sick a second time, and his lifelong friend Brad Green was nursing a throbbing nose, and sulking. Neither man was a graduate student. Brad was the sort of person who picked up and dropped jobs every other week for many reasons which all boiled down to his bad attitude, and Harvey had a steady if low-paying job at a car wash on Amelia Island. The graduate studies in coastal erosion had been a polite fiction cooked up by Professor Willis Griffin so he could bring them along without—he had claimed—having to explain to the college why he was using school property for investigations of a personal nature.

Harvey was starting to wish he had never agreed to come along. Harvey Tanner was not cut out for this sort of thing; he had been encouraged to volunteer his services to Professor Griffin by his now-deceased half brother Cliff Dodson and his friend Brad, after Cliff dazzled Harvey with tales of the vast amounts of money this one academic type was willing to part with for a bit of dirty work and some acting. The idea of killing anyone hadn't occurred to Harvey until Professor Griffin had spelled it out, grimacing in refined distaste the whole time, and then he had been in far too deep to back out. Plus, Brad had insisted that they would probably never even have to do more than push a few teenagers around.

"You don't think they're dead, do you?" Harvey asked Brad for the fifth time. The plan, at least as it had been laid out for Harvey, had been to "accidentally" lock Chris and Carrie Kingsolver in the equipment room while Brad and Harvey helped the professor scout out the site of the lost treasure ship, tell both teenagers that the ship had not been at the coordinates as expected, and then head back to shore. The professor would then get a professional diver and begin excavation of the site, with Brad and Harvey standing guard and getting rewarded handsomely for their assistance. But then Carrie had come out of the bathroom and *looked* at Harvey and somehow seemed to know exactly what the plan was, and in trying to stop her before she warned her cousin, Harvey had chased her onto the deck and then Brad had turned up to help and instead she had gone overboard. And

Harvey knew his friend's temper. Brad might say that Carrie had gone overboard accidentally, but she'd given him a nasty broken nose and he wasn't at all upset about what had happened.

"Oh for—Harv, you better *hope* they are," Brad replied, and Harvey gulped. "Because if they aren't, then we could be on the hook for all sorts of trouble. You'd better believe the professor will blame us and get away scot free."

"What a terrible thing to accuse me of," the professor said right behind Harvey, who jumped.

"He didn't mean it!" Harvey said.

"Of course I did," Brad grumbled. "Harvey, grow a spine and stop whining."

"Ay," the professor agreed, unfolding his arms and revealing that he had a clunky pair of binoculars in one hand. "Although some spineless animals can be quite courageous, this worrying is going to keep you from success. Look at me—I have made incredible and painful sacrifices to get to this moment, but do you see me crying?"

No, they didn't. He had looked after Chris and Carrie as the boat sped away with a calm, thoughtful expression, and when the tiny black specks had disappeared behind them he had turned to Harvey and Brad and told them that it had been terrible, but Carrie had fallen overboard in the rough waters and Chris, "even though Harvey tried to hold him back," had leapt after her. There had been nothing anyone could do. And Chris and Carrie were practically the man's family.

"So we're here, then?" Brad asked while Harvey was trying to remember if he'd ever seen the professor cry or attempt any kind of normal human response to a situation. This was hampered by Harvey having no good idea how to interpret the way Professor Griffin regularly rambled at people. "Looks pretty tame."

"Well, there are hardly going to be dragons here," the professor said, scanning the coastline. "'Here there be dragons,' and all that, but that phrase marked the edge of the world known to mapmakers, and this is quite well charted. Just not quite well charted enough . . . " He trailed off.

"Is something wrong?" Harvey asked. Either the professor or the location itself was scaring him.

"Hmm," said the professor, and went quickly back into the cabin. He was back out a second later, frowning and holding a yellow sticky note. "No," he said. "The coordinates are correct, and Carrie's got lovely, clear handwriting, so there can't be a mistake."

"I take it we're not about to find the lost treasure of the *Sam Elmo*?" Brad asked. The professor didn't seem to hear him. Privately, Harvey thought that was a good thing. The professor didn't look like he was going to take sarcasm very well right now. And the ship was called the *San Telmo,* not the *Sam Elmo.*

"It should be here," the professor said. "It was supposed to be here. They were so close, I could feel it, she can't possibly be wrong, this *has* to be the place!" He picked up the binoculars again and scanned the coastline frantically.

"So, I guess this was a bust," Brad said, stretching and turning in the direction of the cabin.

"*It has to be here!*"

The moon was shimmering on the water, and moonlight shone off a sliver of sand and bounced amongst the tangles of vegetation all along the stretch of shoreline. It was pretty, in an entirely unromantic way, and the boat hugging the edge of the shoreline, light shining warmly from the cabin and small figures standing on the deck, only added to the picture. The screaming coming from the boat would have detracted from the mood quite a bit, had there been anyone nearby to appreciate it.

"Nothing!" Willis Griffin snarled, getting ahold of himself a tiny little bit. "There's nothing *here!*" He was breathing heavily from his session of screaming wordless rage into the night. Harvey was quivering and trying to hide behind Brad, and even Brad looked uncomfortable.

"Well, there's some sand and trees and bushes and stuff," Harvey offered. Griffin rounded on him, ragingly furious, and only backed off when Harvey quailed. Brad, who was still nursing a broken nose and was not in any mood to be charitable, laughed harshly.

"Yeah, tell him, Harvey," he said. "We can make so much money out of all the flipping sand."

"It makes no sense," the professor said, turning the sticky note over and over in his hands. "I was *sure* they'd get it right this time. *She* was sure she had it right this time. It was time for the ship to be found, events conspired to put me in the right place at the right time! All these years, all this waiting, all the hard choices I've made—and can it really all be for nothing?" He crumpled the sticky note and made as if to throw it into the water, but at the last second thought better of it and stuffed the crumpled note into his pocket. "Nothing," he said faintly. There was silence, broken only by the faintest sound of water lapping against the boat. Then the professor's dejected posture straightened, and he lifted his head and set his shoulders and turned to Harvey and Brad.

"Clearly, we missed something," he said decisively, all his old fire and determination back as if he hadn't just had a minor mental breakdown. "We'll just have to turn around and get the children back. I've no doubt Chris will have argued his way to the correct solution by the time we reach them, and we wouldn't want them to get too cold now, would we?"

"Man," Brad said, eying Professor Griffin with caution, "I hate to point out the obvious, but don't you think they're going to be just a bit suspicious of you by now? You did push them overboard and leave them in the middle of the ocean."

"Dear heavens," the professor said, "I had nothing to do with Carrie falling overboard, and it's so hard to steer a ship in this weather." In direct contrast to his words, the ocean was almost eerily calm. "We're awfully lucky that you managed to turn the ship around and remember where they were, aren't we?"

"Sure," Brad muttered under his breath when the professor went to put action to words and turn the ship around. "Whatever you say, crazy man. Oh, stop freaking out," he said to Harvey, who had not stopped shivering. "It's not like this is a haunted ship or anything."

Harvey whimpered and clutched the railing. Going below decks would mean having to look at the scattered possessions of the Kingsolvers, so he stayed where he was, looking out at the dark water and the moon glittering on the surface, all the way back to where the professor had left Chris and Carrie. It was a short trip, since the professor had headed straight out into deeper waters and then straight back in to scan the coastline, so Harvey had only just slipped into an absentminded daydream when Brad and the professor came rushing out on the deck and scared him so badly he almost became the third person to go over the side.

"Well, this is a puzzle," the professor said, peering

over the edge. "I don't see Chris or Carrie, and I don't see what could have taken them, either. Do either of you see any blood in the water, perchance?"

Harvey, who had finally hit his limit, moaned and bolted below decks, where he panicked and locked himself in the equipment room. Brad watched him go with a disgusted sneer, but even he turned to the professor with a look of apprehension.

"Look, I know I told Harvey that the stupid ship wasn't haunted, but you don't think . . . "

"Oh, I always think," the professor replied, still staring at the place where Chris and Carrie should have been, and still frowning. "All the time. Come up with all manner of interesting things."

"Great," Brad grumbled, and was in the middle of turning away to try prying Harvey out of the equipment room when the silence of the night was split by the most unnatural of sounds.

Beedle-beedle-beedle.

Brad whipped his head around in a panic, and

then realized that the sound was more mechanical than supernatural.

Beedle-beedle-beedle.

"Phone!" Brad managed to squeak.

Beedle-beedle-beedle.

"Good heavens!" the professor said, and removed the protesting device from his jacket pocket. "Griffin here," he said, and huffed in relief when he recognized the voice on the other end of the line. "Oh, yes, Aaron, it's good to hear from you. That'll be—*what*?"

The problem with getting a cell phone jammer and using it to prevent your victims from contacting the outside world is, of course, that if you get a cell phone jammer and turn it on then you aren't going to be able to get any of the phone calls sent to your own phone. Professor Griffin hadn't exactly forgotten this, and had in fact counted on it to provide him with an alibi of sorts, since if he were just as cut off from land as Chris and Carrie he would look less like the mastermind and more like a fellow victim. But he had assumed that there would be no urgent calls for him, and that had, perhaps, been a mistake.

"What do you mean, not the only FBI agent in Archer's Grove?" the professor demanded. Brad started edging away, and cast a very thoughtful look at the lifeboat lashed to the deck. The professor saw the look and pulled out his pocketknife, then wandered over to the lifeboat while still on the phone and stabbed the blade of the knife through the bottom of the boat.

"I don't see why you didn't just tell them that there have been reports of a serial killer going around impersonating a federal agent," he said calmly when he was done. "You could have killed two birds with one stone. Did you at least tell someone that McRae was a person of interest in the case?"

Brad looked from the professor to the ruined lifeboat and decided to join Harvey in hiding.

"Well, then what am I paying you for?" the professor asked irritably. "No, no, I'll deal with this. You can't possibly do what I need, and I highly doubt you have the skillset needed to rid me of the naturalist or that troublesome priest. Yes. Goodbye." He hung up the phone with a sigh. "It's as though everyone's against me today," he said to himself, and pulled his pocketknife free of the lifeboat.

CHAPTER TEN

MR. LYNDON HAD GOTTEN THEM A HORRIFYINGLY rough redeye flight, and Maddison's family landed in Tampa, Florida, at the hideously unnatural hour of four a.m. Maddison hadn't gotten much sleep the previous night, and had been on far more airplane flights in the past week than she usually went on in a year, and was thoroughly exhausted and mildly jet-lagged as a result.

"It's surprising they even let us go through with the flight," Maddison's mom said as they peered around a line of grumpy passengers waiting to disembark. "It was so rough they never turned off the Fasten Seatbelts sign."

"At least we'll be home in a bit," Maddison said. She had pulled her phone out the second they started letting people off the plane, horrifying time of night or not, and still couldn't reach Chris. It rang out more than once before it went to voicemail this time though, and Maddison wasn't sure if that was a promising sign or not. She'd been assuming that the phone just wasn't getting service in the middle of the ocean, but Chris should still be out on a boat—so why was his phone doing something different now? She couldn't make sense of it.

Actually, what if there had been a *manufactured* problem with the phone itself, like someone deliberately making it hard for Chris to get in contact with anyone . . .

"How hard would it be to block a cell phone signal?" Maddison asked her mom.

"Moving," her mom said, tapping Maddison on the shoulder, because the line exiting the plane was in fact moving, and Maddison had to put the phone away to exit the plane. "I would imagine it's fairly easy," her mom added as she swung her backpack out of the overhead compartment. "But it might not be the best idea to talk about jamming cell phones in the middle of an airport. Now, see if you can find your father."

They hadn't gotten seats together because the tickets had been so last minute, and it took forever for Maddison and her mom to find her dad in the airport terminal. He had been sitting towards the front of the plane rather than in the second-to-last row, and had already gotten off and then wandered across the airport in search of a restroom and a coffee.

"Dad, it's four in the morning," Maddison said when she caught up to him, parked on an airport bench sipping a large coffee with deep concentration. "Do you really want coffee this early? Or this late, whichever?"

"Do you want me to accidentally sleep-drive us into the Atlantic Ocean?" her dad asked, tilting his head back to rest it against the wall and staring at the ceiling. "Huh," he said, straightening up. "Hey, Mads?"

"What?" There was a strangely amused expression on her father's face that didn't bode well for her future.

"Do me a huge favor and don't make a scene, okay?"

"Why would I make a scene?" Maddison asked. And who would care? The airport was basically dead at going-on-five o'clock and the only people in the terminal were Maddison's family, a cluster of high school students wearing matching orange shirts, and a dark-haired woman with her own cup of coffee who had been leaning against a decorative pillar and studying everyone with one critical eye. Her other eye was fixed on the air conditioner duct on the ceiling.

She glanced up and towards them at about the same time Maddison did and tossed the coffee cup into a trashcan, then started towards Maddison and her dad. Either that, or the gift kiosk next to them, but she didn't look like the type to want a stuffed alligator wearing a straw hat.

"Because you are a very a passionate girl and you have a temper," her dad said, getting to his feet and handing his own cup of coffee to Maddison. "And I think I'm about to be arrested."

"*What?*"

"Impressive," the dark-haired woman said, pausing right in front of them. "Officially, yes, that's exactly what's about to happen. I'm going to walk you out the side door to the police cruiser I have waiting, and my partner"—she looked behind her, frowned, and scanned the terminal until a young man with an orange-striped tie came hurrying over and skidded to a stop next to her—"Forrest," she said firmly, "is going to collect your family and their things and follow us."

"Unofficially, there's a significant danger that someone might try to attack your father and we're attempting to take steps to minimize the danger," Forrest explained when they were all in the car and the windows were rolled up. "He was a person of interest in a missing-persons investigation twenty-five years ago, and the case is being opened again because of recent events involving a church and a dead body. Detective Hermann thought it wisest to pander to the killer, at least for now, so we're letting him think your father is a suspect."

The police station, when Forrest escorted them in, was a scene of complete chaos, Maddison's father and Agent Grey calm islands in the middle of it.

"We've got another situation," Agent Grey said to Forrest. "Or, well, part of one. A Harvey Tanner just reported two teenagers lost at sea. The idiot called one of the families, bawling, and tried to confess, so we have a riot on our hands."

Maddison sat down hard on a nearby desk.

"And to make matters worse, we've also just gotten a report that both kids are fine, if a little cold and shaken, and if we want to catch Griffin in the act we need to suppress that report before he realizes what's happened."

"So, Chris and Carrie are okay?" Maddison asked. Then it occurred to her that the two FBI agents might not be able to tell her much, if anything, and she amended it to "Please just tell me if they're safe?"

"They seem to be?" Forrest said, squinting at a transcript like he wasn't sure it was real.

"Oh heavens," Maddison's father said suddenly, and without warning he began to laugh. Real, deep laughter, edging into hysteria. "Of course! He would get himself mixed up in all this, almost completely by accident, coming in at the very last minute to save the day while babbling."

"Who?"

"Robin Wyzowski," her dad said, shaking his head. Forrest blinked, tilted his head to one side, and finally checked something on his phone.

"That's . . . completely accurate," he said, impressed. "Saved by Robin Wyzowski."

"How is Robin Wyzowski mixed up in all this?" Maddison asked, because she knew who Robin

Wyzowski was to her dad but there was an undertone to the conversation she was missing.

"He has always had the most amazing ability to find weirdness," her father explained, still laughing.

✗ ✗ ✗

Meanwhile, out in the Atlantic Ocean, with the lights of Archer's Grove sparkling in the distance, Robin Redd looked up from trying to make Chris and Carrie hot chocolate and made a face.

"My ears are burning," he said. Bethy automatically looked at his head in alarm, because he had in fact once caught his ears on fire by standing too close to a candelabra, but he was mercifully flame-free. This she pointed out, on the off chance that he didn't know.

"Would it be more accurate to say that someone just walked over my grave?" Redd asked. "Or, hmm, that there's a pricking in my thumbs?"

"Something wicked this way comes," Carrie

finished automatically. She and Chris were curled together at the boat's tiny table, wrapped in blankets and still dripping slightly on the floor. "Shakespeare, *Macbeth*. Is something coming?" She didn't know how much more she could handle tonight. It had been a lucky chance that had brought the *Meandering Manatee* close enough to where Chris and Carrie were bobbing in the water to see them, and an even more massive stroke of luck that had given Carrie the courage to flag down the bizarre little ship. With multicolored Christmas lights reflecting crazily off the lavender hull and a crimson deck and a life-sized purple inflatable manatee dangling crazily from the hook, intended as a windsock, the *Manatee* looked like a ship from the depths of Hell itself. Then Robin Redd had leaned over the side, recognized Chris and Carrie, and yelled a "Hello!" and the ship suddenly looked welcoming. Not that Carrie wasn't afraid Redd was going to poison them with the hot chocolate he was trying to make, using the remnants of someone's mixed-value pack of Hershey's bite-sized chocolates and a carton of soy milk.

"Nothing's coming, except for a storm front this Thursday," Redd said. "But I feel as though somewhere out there, someone is talking about me," he explained, whisking industriously. Carrie had watched him drop several Hershey's almond bars in the saucepan, so she doubted he was getting rid of all the lumps even if he whisked for the rest of the night. "Or perhaps they're taking my name in vain. It's hard to tell when your worst episode ever has become a meme."

As one, the camera crew, Bethy, and Flo groaned "Muskrat Dinner." Although Flo was stuck in a perpetual state of horror at the sight of what Redd was doing to a handful of innocent chocolate bars.

"Do I even want to know?" Carrie asked Chris, who had watched more episodes of *Robin Redd: Treasure Hunter* than she had.

"Did you know," Chris asked from his nest of blankets, "that some Catholic churches in Minnesota and surrounding states have muskrat dinners during Lent?"

"Right," Carrie said, "I did not want to know—Redd, aren't you used to people talking about you? You have your own television show."

"I don't use my given name for the show," Redd explained. "It's too embarrassing, and I like being anonymous."

Nobody pointed out that someone who naturally dressed and acted like his television persona was hardly being anonymous, but Redd said, "I have a double life," defensively anyway.

"I only ever feel my ears burn when someone is talking about me using my given name," Redd explained, giving the hot chocolate a final whisk and tipping the contents into cups. "It's much more serious an occasion, there are only ten or twelve people who know—anyone else want some of this?" he offered. There was not a sudden rush.

"Oh, here," Bethy sighed when he started to looked dejected, handing the first two cups to Chris and Carrie and cautiously taking a third when Redd offered it to her. "You were saying?" The hot chocolate was definitely hot, and also definitely had some chocolate in it, so technically it fit the definition. Even if it did taste strangely like strawberries.

"Only ten or twelve people know that I was born Robin Wyzowski," Redd finished. Carrie swallowed her mouthful of hot chocolate too fast and started coughing. "And now almost twenty of them do," Redd added thoughtfully, sipping his own hot chocolate. "I'm not sure that's a good thing. Nobody takes me seriously when my name is Wyzowski, it's probably why nobody believed me when I tried to help give Kevin an alibi during that business with Ryan."

"I'll take you seriously," Carrie offered, still coughing. Somehow the name fit him.

"Thank you," Redd said, and then took a deep gulp of his drink and made a strangled *urk* noise.

"Redd!" Bethy gasped. He was making the most amazing faces.

"I think that all the nuts from the chocolate bars

settled at the bottom," Redd said faintly once he'd taken several deep breaths and blown his nose.

"Why me?" Bethy muttered, burying her head in her hands.

"Otherwise, this worked really well," Redd added, studying his cup. "I'll have to make this kind of hot chocolate again some time." This time it was Flo who made a horrified noise.

"Don't," Bethy said, not looking up. "Flo might actually throw you overboard and we've had enough people go overboard tonight."

"Yes, that would put a damper on the evening."

"I'm damp," Chris said glumly. "And still a little confused."

"I just can't believe you actually took that inflatable manatee on the boat," Bethy mumbled, "and that it actually made the boat look frightening from an angle, and that anyone would think this ship was haunted. This ship would be an insult to all haunted ships!"

Carrie blushed and took a sip of her hot chocolate

to cover it up. The manatee had looked just enough like a person floating in mid-air to scare her. Up close, the only thing scary about it was the painted doe-eyes.

"You keep telling me the *San Telmo* isn't a haunted ship," Bethy added. "But ever since you mentioned the name we've been followed by strange events—which I guess would make it more of a cursed ship than a haunted ship."

"Oh, that's the great trick of the *San Telmo*," Redd explained. "It's not a haunted ship, but it's the sort of ship that haunts your whole life if you aren't careful."